TAKING BABY FOR A WALK

KATHRYN GOSSOW

Published by Odyssey Books in 2021

www.odysseybooks.com.au

A Cataloguing-in-Publication entry is available from the National Library of Australia

ISBN: 978-1-922311-36-8 (pbk)

ISBN: 9978-1-922311-37-5 (ebook)

Cover design by Michelle Lovi

Cover image from Adobe Stock

SUNDAY

Baby wants to go for a walk.

Bree-Anna, hands on hips, tells Baby, 'You just have to wait.'

Baby wails and whines. Bree-Anna sighs, picks Baby up from her cot, wags her finger and says, 'Shut up, or I will give you something to cry about.'

She walks the small circle of her bedroom and rocks Baby, back and forth. Baby's eyes click open and closed. One of them gets stuck, and Bree-Anna unsticks it with her finger. *Click.* Open. *Click.* Close.

'Rock-a-bye baby on the treetop, when the wind blows, the cradle will rock, when the bough breaks the cradle will fall,'

Bree-Anna drops Baby.

'...and down will come baby...'

She catches Baby just before she hits the ground.

'...cradle and all.'

This is their game. It scares Baby, but being scared makes you braver.

Baby's big painted eyes stare back at Bree-Anna. Her mouth, stuck smiling forever, smiles at her. Bree-Anna's belly rumbles like a train. She dangles Baby by her arm and lets Baby's face bang onto her leg as she wanders into the kitchen.

On the table, on Mummy's plate, last night's chicken nuggets and chips sit globby and cold. Mummy hardly ever finishes her food. Bree-Anna pokes it, moves a nugget around on the plate, wondering how it will taste, but then sees the red blobs of chilli sauce. Chilli sauce makes her tongue burn fire. It might be funny to make Baby eat it, but she won't be mean today. Not like Declan. Declan put chilli sauce all over her hotdog and told her it was special tomato sauce. Then he said, *Here, drink this,* and gave her water. That was wrong, wrong, wrong and even meaner. Mummy laughed too and said she should have milk; water just makes it burn worser. Bree-Anna wanted to pinch Declan. Squeeze his skin between her fingers and twist it.

Declan only cares about Pokémon. Pokémon is more stupider than vegetables.

In the cupboard, she finds an open packet with two biscuits, the sort with orange icing in them. She plops onto the floor, Baby on her lap. Baby doesn't like the orange icing, so Bree-Anna eats them both.

The special thing about today is Rachel's party. The hands on the clock point with the big hand to the three and the little hand to the number with two ones. She counts all the numbers until she gets to eleven to remember its name. The invitation stuck to the fridge tells the time of the party. She stretches to reach and pulls the invitation down, touches the wings of the pretty pink fairies, bumpy with glue and glitter. She opens it and tries to read the time, but it is written in letters instead of numbers.

Declan's in the loungeroom (as usual) playing Pokémon (as usual). She climbs onto the couch and sits Baby between them. The Christmas tree's lights blink, blink, but she can hardly see their colours for the bright sun shining through the window.

'What time is the party?'

Declan's fingers fly all over the buttons. Bree-Anna wants to be fast like him, but not with a stupid game like Pokémon. At the shopping centre she asked Santa for an iPad for Christmas and she said—just to make sure he knew—*no* Pokémon.

Bree-Anna's thumb pops into her mouth. One minute she is talking, the next minute she is sucking. She's not a baby. She's five now. Too big for sucking thumbs, but sometimes her thumb has a mind of its own. Lucky Mummy is not here to slap her hand, and her fingers smell good, better than Declan. He stinks bad, dirty clothes bad.

Her thumb pops when she pulls it out. She likes that noise, *pop, pop, pop.*

'Stop making that stupid noise,' Declan says.

'What time does it say?' She waves the invitation in his face.

He twists away and swings his game and knocks Baby over. 'I'm in the middle of a battle... If you make me lose...'

'You stink!' Bree-Anna jumps off the couch and pulls Baby by her leg. She tries to stomp across the carpet, but it's squishy and doesn't make angry noises.

They stop outside Mummy's room. Bree-Anna puts on her extra good hearing ears. Sometimes when Mummy wakes up, she stays in bed and does Facebook with her phone. She touches the doorknob. She turns the knob without opening it, moving it just a little so maybe Mummy might see and call out to come in. She doesn't.

'Mummy,' Bree-Anna whispers.

Being scared makes you braver, so she turns the knob all the way. The door opens a tiny crack. The air-conditioner hums quietly like a sleeping bear, and cold air tickles her feet. She goes tippy-toe through the gap in the door. The closed curtains make the room dark, almost like night, but she has eagle eyes. Mummy says she always finds the lost things in the house.

She creeps closer. Her heart does a frightened jump. There are two shapes in the bed.

The man's shoulder sticks up like a mountain. She can't climb over it to get to Mummy. Mummy's jammed right up against the wall. The man takes over the whole bed. She doesn't know where he came from, but then the mans turn up like that sometimes, especially after Mummy has a 'night out'. Sometimes they are nice.

Baby and Bree-Anna kneel at the end of the bed. She pushes her chin into the hard edge of the mattress. Her tummy gurgles loud and the man moves. *Be quiet, Baby*, she tells Baby, but only with her head, not with her tongue. Special Magic Powers let her talk with Baby like that.

Mummy's feet are little lumps under the sheet, though she can't tell which end are her toes. She reaches toward them. If Mummy gets angry, Bree-Anna will blame Declan because he won't tell her the time and she doesn't know when to get ready for Rachel's party.

'Mummy, wake up,' she whispers with her mouse voice. She wishes she had Magic Powers to talk with Mummy with her head instead of her mouth, like she does with Baby. She taps Mummy's foot. 'Rachel's party is today.'

Mummy is a sleepy head duffer. Last time, when Lauren had a party, they got so late Bree-Anna missed the pizza and pass-the-parcel. The pass-the-parcel prize was a whole block of chocolate.

The man rises up, and she sees he is the troll man! He grins at Bree-Anna with crooked teeth and his hair like a dirty, ugly mop. Bree-Anna snatches Baby up by her hair and crawls on her hands and knees, dragging Baby, *bump, bump*, along the carpet.

She crawls all the way down the hall, across the kitchen lino and into her room. She pushes the door closed and leans up against it so the troll can't get inside. The troll came into her room once. That's how she knows he is a monster who pretends to be a man. Not like Shrek. He's an ogre. Like the troll under the bridge that eats little girls all up.

She hugs Baby close. 'Don't cry, Baby. I've put a force field on the door. See?' She holds her up and shows her the door. Baby keeps crying and if she keeps crying the troll will hear her and the force field isn't real. Just pretend.

'Shush,' she says with her voice like Mummy's when she's mad. Baby stops crying and Bree-Anna leaves her on the floor to think about what she's done.

Bree-Anna's tummy rumbles, still hungry. She leans heavy as she can on the door. At Rachel's party will be lollies and chips. Then Bree-Anna has a bright idea, like a lightbulb going *pop* in her head—just like in cartoons. 'Let's go for a walk. To Rachel's house!' she tells Baby.

She drags her dollhouse in front of the door to keep out the troll and dresses in her pink shorts and the new pink T-shirt. Mummy got it for her yesterday. The T-shirt says 'princess' in silver letters.

'See,' she shows Baby the princess words, 'P for princess. It matches my doona cover.' She points to the bed. Baby can't see the princess on the doona because of too much mess, but talking takes Baby's mind off the troll.

She puts Baby in her stroller and she doesn't even complain. Bree-Anna tries to tuck a blanket over Baby, but Baby tells her it's hot outside and remember yesterday was *hot as Hades*. That's what Mummy said. She said Hades is where Bree-Anna's dad is.

Rachel's present fits in the basket under the stroller's seat. Mummy didn't have time to help her wrap it because she had to do her make-up for her night out. Bree-Anna wrapped it all by herself, but not very well. The wrapping's corners stick out crooked. Inside is a necklace and a bracelet. Mummy helped her pick them. They are pink because Rachel loves pink. Bree-Anna loves pink too.

Bree-Anna drags the dollhouse away and opens the door real slow and peeks down the hall. Her heart thumps and she hopes Baby can't hear it. The troll is nowhere in sight.

She wheels Baby into the kitchen and calls to Declan. 'I'm taking Baby for a walk.' She doesn't really want him to hear her because he will say they can't go, but she will get in trouble if she doesn't tell him. She leaves fast out the back door before he can say stop. Outside, her new pink thongs are waiting for her. They have plastic yellow flowers on them. She puts them on her feet and they make her smile.

Baby was right about not needing the blanket. The sun goes *bang, bang, bang* on her head. She pushes the stroller through the long grass at the side of the house and stops on the footpath. Sweat sticks between her legs and under her arms.

She looks back at the house, up the street and then down at Baby. 'Let's go,' she says, and they set off down the footpath.

Everyone must still be in bed or in their houses because it is too hot to come out. Even the birds are quiet today. 'It's like everyone is dead,' she says to Baby, and then she wishes she didn't because Baby gets scared again.

At the end of the cul-de-sac, she lifts the wire fence and they squeeze under. She pushes the stroller along the old track toward the cow paddock and the service station. Sometimes Mummy sends her and Declan down the track to buy milk and bread at the servo, and lollies or ice-cream if there is change left over.

They stop near the cows. Baby likes to say hello to them. She won't touch them because they are big and brown and dirty and it's good they are on the other side of the fence, but she likes to watch them chomping on grass. The sun blasts off the servo's driveway and Baby says, *Keep walking, it's too hot to stop*. Bree-Anna looks behind her because she thinks maybe Declan might have followed, but he isn't there. She wheels the stroller down the track and turns onto the highway. Sweat runs down her back and her hair sticks to her head like glue. Her tongue feels like she ate a sandpit. When she gets to Rachel's, the first thing she is going to do is get a big cold drink!

Pushing the stroller beside the highway is a hard old slog, as her grandma would say. She stoops lower and heaves through the deep dirt and big rocks that turn the wheels the wrong way. If she pushes all the way to the school, they can use the crossing and that will be safer. Bree-Anna hopes it will be easy to find Rachel's house with the big red letterbox. It will probably have balloons on it too. Pink ones.

Dirt gets into her thongs and the new stiff plastic rubs between her toes. She wipes sweat away from her eyes. Maybe she should have waited for Mummy to drive. *You dumb cow, Bree-Anna. You are the dumbest thing ever born. You should have waited.* Baby doesn't say that. Bree-Anna says it to herself. She doesn't need Baby to tell her and Baby just clucks her tongue. A truck swoops by and almost knocks her over with its wind. The prickly grass scratches her legs and she wonders if there might be snakes. She looks behind her, the servo hidden by the curve in the road. No Declan.

The car comes suddenly and stops right in their way so they can't keep walking. It's the froggy car. Baby and Bree-Anna call it the froggy car because of it being green like a frog.

The froggy car man crawls over to the passenger side, winds down the window, leans half his body out of the opening, and says, 'That looks like hard work.'

Bree-Anna nods. She shoves the stroller out of the dirt hole it's in. She can't see how to get past the car.

'Where you going all on your own?'

'A party,' she says, her voice croaky.

'Oh! I'm going to a party. Is it the same one?'

'Rachel's?' The sun burns on the back of Bree-Anna's neck.

'Yes, Rachel's party. Why don't we go together?' he says, opening the car door and climbing out. He holds the door open for her. 'You can sit in the front with me. I'll do it as a favour, for your mum. She wouldn't like to see you out here all hot and pushing that doll.'

Bree-Anna wipes the sweat from her upper lip and checks on Baby. She wishes Baby would say something about the man and the froggy car.

'Come on,' he says. 'Your mum won't mind. She told me I should look out for you. You don't want to miss the party.'

She takes Baby out of the stroller. Baby is boiling hot. He picks up the stroller and grins at Bree-Anna. She crawls in the front seat, clutching Baby, and before she can think or look, he slams the door closed.

He gets into the driver's seat and takes off, car wheels skidding in the dust. She sits up on her knees and looks behind them. Baby's stroller is still on the side of the road.

'Rachel's present,' she says.

He grips the steering wheel, stares straight ahead.

They fly past the school and the right past the turn he should take to Rachel's street.

'Go back,' she says.

But he doesn't.

Petrol fumes plunge like a fist into the back of Jake's throat. He swallows them down with thick saliva.

Today is the last day he should have let himself have a hangover.

He thumps the pump nozzle into the tank, his fist clenched. His eyes squint against the searing light. Petrol gushes into the empty tank and tar-thick vapour punches him again. He turns away and leans his head against his dust-caked car. His head throbs. A bulldozer moves his brains about.

Heat pummels the pitted bitumen. The town is a dump. He understands now why Carla hated the place. Stinky Gully is nothing but a crappy little highway town, good for nothing except cheap petrol. Well, less expensive petrol. That bitch didn't know what it cost him to visit. Five hours driving and another half hour to go. Then back again for the midnight shift. Casual workers like him got all the crap shifts.

She better not give him trouble today. Who was he kidding? She always gives him trouble!

In the paddock next to the petrol station, mangy cattle whack flies with their tails. Cheap brick houses litter this part of town. They are silent today, like tombs baking in the heat.

Jake wipes sweat from his upper lip, glances at the litres ticking over, the dollars mounting up. The highway grumbles, vacant and broiling.

A little girl wanders along a rutted track between the petrol station and the paddock. In Jake's school days, they would have called her fat. But these days you see fatter. She's about the same age as La-Li.

La-Li. He smiles to himself. His girl, sweet and sugary, like spearmint lollies.

The girl stops to pick her too-tight pink shorts from her bum. She has a toy stroller, the plastic legs of a doll twisting out of it toward the sky. The girl looks behind her, as though for a lagging parent. Then she bends and coos over the doll. Stands. Tugs her pink T-shirt over her pudgy belly and pushes the stroller through a pothole in the path.

The pump clicks, finished. Eighty-two friggin' dollars.

The girl in pink turns off the path and weaves her stroller through the dirt alongside the highway. Jake looks back up the empty path behind her. No one is there.

Inside the cool of the petrol station, Jake ignores the tongs and uses his hands to toss two sausage rolls in a paper bag. He stands a while in the open door of the icy fridge before he gets a Coke.

'Gonna be a hot one,' the cashier says, lifting himself from against the wall near the cash register.

'Hot already, mate,' Jake says. He searches through the large window, between the advertisements for Cadbury chocolate and firewood. 'Did you see that little girl? The one with the doll?' he asks.

'Nah.' The cashier swipes the Coke. Sparse hairs, like struggling seedlings, grow on his upper lip. 'Cash or card?' He holds out his hand.

Back in his car, Jake blasts the air-con onto high and bites into a sausage roll. Flakes of pastry fall on his lap. He sucks air through his mouth and rolls the too-hot food off his tongue. Just what the doctor ordered. Food in one hand, steering wheel in the other, he bumps over the ditched driveway onto the highway.

A few hundred metres ahead of him, a lime-green station wagon has pulled over, its arse-end hanging skew-whiff half on the road. Dickhead. Jake manoeuvres around the vehicle. Who would own a car that colour? He glances in the rear-view mirror.

The little girl in pink is climbing into the passenger seat. The clock on the dash tells Jake he is late. Carla will have his balls for breakfast. He peers back in the mirror, but he can't see the lime-green car for the bend in the road. He accelerates, turns up the volume: the Chilli Peppers, *Californication*. His fingers twitch to the beat. The rear-view mirror reveals empty road. The station wagon isn't following.

Bree-Anna shrinks back in the seat and hugs Baby close to her chest. She talks to Baby, the quiet Magic whisper with her mind. *Now, Baby, don't you be a scaredy-cat. Mr Randall will take us to the party. Mummy and Declan will get your stroller back. No one will steal it, I promise and promise, cross my heart and hope to die.* She crosses her heart with her fingers.

'Get down,' Mr Randall says, his teeth tight together. Bree-Anna hugs Baby closer and Baby's stiff fingers stab into her chest. Mr Randall twists his hands around and around the steering wheel. His knuckles stick up, pointy and white.

'You want to surprise your friend?' He smiles, but his voice doesn't sound excited like a surprise is coming. 'Well, *get down!*' He grabs her shoulder with his fingers digging in and shoves her down. She crumples down onto the floor. Fat tears come to her eyes, but she keeps them in so as not to worry Baby. The floor smells like a wet bath mat and makes vomit come up in her mouth. Her heart thumps and probably even Baby can hear it. *We're going the long way around,* she tells Baby in her silent voice. *We're going to give Rachel the biggest surprise ever.*

Mr Randall drives fast, the car skids around a corner, and they roll around on the dirty floor, bits of yucky things sticking to her legs. They might have an accident, she thinks, and she's not wearing a seatbelt. Mummy always makes her wear a seat-belt. Mummy says you might die in an accident if you aren't wearing a seatbelt. Mr Randall might have an accident. She might die!

The car slows down, and she hears stones spit up under it like they are on a dirt road, like the road when they go to visit Grandma. The car stops and Bree-Anna smashes her head. The bang knocks out her tears. She tries to drag them back inside, but they have escaped. What will she tell Rachel about the present? *This is Rachel's house.* She squeezes Baby. *Stop saying it isn't.*

She wants to get off the floor, away from the dirt and yuck sticking to them and the smell of old wet. Baby wants to get out of the car and find out where they are, if they are near to home, or at Rachel's house. *This is a different way to get to Rachel's.* She smacks Baby's bottom, but not hard. *We are on the floor so we can surprise Rachel. Jump out. Happy Birthday! Surprise!*

Mr Randall looks down at them. His eyes pop out of his eye-holes like balloons squeezed tight in a fist, going to burst. 'Shut your eyes,' he says, and she does and she hopes Baby does too. She squishes herself tight in the corner. She works hard to keep her eyelids closed. Tears squeeze out the gaps she can't close up. The car door opens and bangs shut and she flicks her eyes open. Her breath runs in and out like when she races at school, but they have just been here on the floor, not moving at all.

The door next to her opens, and she closes her eyes again and tells Baby, *Close your eyes.*

'Don't look,' he says, and she's glad she told Baby that already.

She forces her eyelids down tighter and tighter so they don't snap open. She doesn't know what will happen if she opens her eyes. She doesn't know why she keeps them closed. She feels his hands on her tummy, yanking, trying to pull her out of her corner.

'Come on,' he grumbles, and his breath smells eggy. He jabs

his thumbs into her sides and she lets him lift her out of the car. Her thongs fall off, and her knees bang on something hard, and he doesn't care. He isn't careful. A sob comes out of her mouth. He holds her against him, Baby pressed between them. He twists his arms around her, pushes her face into his shoulder and holds her head there, her face jammed right into him, and she can feel the sticky sweat on his neck and smell his dirty clothes. The car door slams and his feet crunch over the ground. Bree-Anna feels the scratchy of Baby's hair on her chin. He carries them up long stairs. There aren't any stairs at Rachel's house. She wants to kick her legs to get down, but she is too scared. She hears keys rattling and the crunching of the lock. She peeks and sees a door, green paint peeling, and he opens the door, and she closes her eyes again.

Inside, he drops her onto something soft. She bounces. A lounge, she thinks, and she makes herself small in a ball and puts her thumb in her mouth and sucks hard, crying, but quiet so he doesn't hear her. The cushion smells like sick and scratches her cheek. Baby presses into her and says *I told you so*, but Bree-Anna already knows, and Baby can't help.

She can hear him stomping back and forth, back and forth, and saying bad words like shit and worse words like the one that is the f word. She curls up smaller than a centipede.

He stomps back and forth and back and forth and then he says, 'You hungry?'

She was a long time ago, but now she can't eat anything. She shakes her head.

'Speak up,' he says and pulls her up to sit and her eyes pop open and she wishes they didn't. She huddles back into the cushion, sucks her thumb and smells the familiar of her own skin, fights the fresh tears in her eyes.

'Cat got your tongue? You hungry or not? You want eggs? I got eggs.'

She shakes her head again.

'Speak.' He wraps his knobbly hand around her wrist and yanks her thumb, *pop*, out of her mouth. 'Speak.'

'No,' she says. The tiny word gets stuck in her throat and she can hardly hear it at all.

'No what? Where's your manners?'

'No, thank you,' she chokes out louder.

He stands up and cracks his knuckles, *crunch*, like a branch breaking apart, and says, 'Don't move,' and leaves. She hears clanging in a room behind her and she knows he is in the kitchen making eggs. She hates eggs.

She wraps herself like a blanket around Baby, shoves her thumb into her mouth again, and she thinks Mummy wouldn't care, that it would be one of those times when she would be allowed to have it in her mouth. She thinks she will strangle Baby, she holds her so tight. But Baby doesn't complain. Baby would suck her thumb too, if she could.

Curtains cover the windows, like Mummy's room, except instead of being cool with the air-conditioner, the air is like hot bath water, and she can hardly breathe at all.

When she hears him walking back in the room, her heart thumps faster. He sits on the floor in front of her, his legs crossed. His shorts are too big for his skinny legs and Bree-Anna can see the hairy white inside bits of his body.

'I am not going to hurt you,' he says. Bits of egg sandwich fall out of his mouth as he talks. She sucks her thumb, her teeth in her knuckle, her tongue tight over her fingernail. Her nose runs and she lets the snot run down over her fist.

'I am not one of those kiddie fuckers—oops.' His hand covers his mouth, and then he takes it away and grins, sandwich all over his teeth. 'Sorry I swore. I don't have intercourse with children.'

She doesn't know what he means, but she thinks maybe it is

like the mans who stay in Mummy's bed sometimes. Or like the troll that time in her room.

She doesn't want to look at the egg on his teeth or hear the words he is talking. He sits on the floor, swaying back and forth, his mouth chewing, his jaw big and sharp.

There was a thing on her curtain once, in her bedroom. It swayed back and forth, not going anywhere, standing still, moving and swaying. She thought it would jump on her and its skinny long legs would crawl on her skin. She screamed. Mummy said she was a silly duffer and it was just a stick insect.

Bree-Anna didn't know how a stick could come alive like that, grow bulgy eyes and long legs. Maybe Mr Randall has something to do with it, because he is long and bumpy, like a stick. Maybe he will jump on her and touch her with his stick fingers and maybe freeze her into a twig.

Declan's brave with insects and bugs. He let the stick insect walk onto his arm. He said he would take it outside, but first he tried to put it on her! After that she got scared that a whole tree could come alive. That it would come into her room and crush her to death. Mummy said that's silly, trees don't come alive like that—but yes, they do. They come alive and they are Mr Randall. Just like a big stick monster.

The gate hangs off its hinges, and Jake must lift it so that it doesn't scrape over the concrete path. Marigolds, orange and yellow as the sunshine, line the path, mocking him with their brightness.

Jake climbs the long stairs, his heart thumping. He stops at the top to kick and test the wobble of the loose tread. He crosses the veranda and raps the fist-shaped brass knocker.

Realising his hand is clenched, he releases it, stretches his fingers, and breathes deeply.

From inside the house comes the sound of clanging cutlery thrown into a drawer, the radio drone of a man's voice. Radio National. Culture and philosophy or some daft thing.

Jake shifts his weight from one leg to the other. Taps his hand against his thigh.

The *crunch* of crockery.

The *thump* of a cupboard door closing.

Damn her.

He bangs the knocker again, harder, louder. Flecks of paint rain down off the door.

Footsteps thud down the hall and the door flings open.

'You're late.'

Only fifteen minutes! 'Traffic,' Jake says. He peers past her shoulder into the shadowed house.

She blocks the doorway, her hand pressed on the door jamb. 'There's no traffic Sundays.'

'Daddy, Daddy, Daddy.' La-Li's footsteps are like music on the floorboards. She ducks under her mother's arm. Jake bends to one knee and his girl falls into him and he melts. Squeezing her close, he breathes her in. She smells different. Like margarine.

She wriggles from his grasp. 'It's only four sleeps till Santa comes. We put up the tree.' She tugs at his hand. 'Come see. Come see.'

Carla, his wife—his ex-wife—rests her hand on the girl's head. 'Go now. Daddy and I have to talk.'

'But Muuum.' La-Li stamps her foot.

'Go and get ready,' her mother says in a stern voice.

'I *am* ready.'

'Just for a minute, La-Li, one minute,' Jake says, patting her hair flat and smooth. He rises from his stoop, his knees creak.

La-Li's blue eyes plead with her mother. Jake's blue eyes. Proof that she is his.

'Go on, get,' Carla says.

La-Li stomps into the house.

'Her name is *not* La-Li.' Carla crosses her short arms across her chest. Her too-short arms and broad shoulders make Jake think of the dinosaur in *Toy Story*.

Jake's hangover headache crushes his temples. 'She likes it when I call her La-Li.'

'It sounds like the name an Asian hooker would use.'

'Your feminist friends think it's all right to say things like that?' he replies.

She glares at him. 'We named her Alannah-Lily. Remember? Remember *that* day?'

He remembers agreeing to Alannah Lily. The hyphen was never discussed. The hyphen was a joke. The hyphen was the reason for La-Li.

'I remember,' he sighs.

She spins and enters the house. He steps over the unfamiliar threshold and follows. She's had her hair done. Dyed into the back of her short hair is leopard print. Brown, black, and blond. So that is where his child support payment goes. He realises the hair matches her leopard print dress. Tattooed birds fly down the back of her round arms. They fly, he knows, from a jungle of roses across her shoulder blades. Lust surprises him.

The kitchen bench is littered with crumbs. He leans against it and watches her hang cups on cup hooks. 'You're looking well,' he says.

She turns to face him. 'What are you doing with her?'

He has an unexpected flash of the little girl in pink picking her shorts from her bum.

'Who?'

'Alannah-Lily. Where are you taking her?'

'Oh.' Jake exhales a gushing breath. 'I thought we'd go to the park. Get some lunch.'

'I don't want her playing on the slide.'

'The slide? You mean the slippery dip? What's wrong with the slippery dip?'

'They said it on the radio. Fourteen percent of paediatric leg fractures in toddlers are caused by slides.'

'La—Alannah-Lily isn't a toddler anymore.'

'Do you *want* to take her out?' she says, pronouncing each word slowly.

'No slippery dips,' he says.

'And I don't want her eating rubbish. McDonald's is out. KFC is out. Go to the café on Limestone Street. Alannah-Lily likes the mini quiches, or they do sandwiches. Do not order the chicken nuggets. Do not order the chips. They are full of trans fats, saturated fat, and salt.'

Jake makes a noise he hopes sounds like a helicopter.

'What?' She lunges toward him, her eyes round, her stocky body voluptuous in wildcat print.

'It's probably not even chicken,' Jake says, calmly wiping the bench-top crumbs from his hands. 'If that's everything, we'll head off.' He strides across the kitchen and calls down the hall. 'Let's go.'

'Wait,' Carla demands from behind him.

He twists, ready to face off with her.

She holds out a tube of sunscreen. 'Make sure she wears it.'

He snatches the sunscreen. La-Li runs into the back of his knees and hugs his thighs to her face. He bends down and picks her up to his hip. She clings to his neck with one hand and clutches a Barbie doll with the other hand. She kisses his cheek. 'Daddy, can we go to McDonald's again?'

'We'll see.' He kisses her shoulder. Pale and soft as sponge cake. 'You got your hat?'

They stop at the corner store. He holds La-Li over the freezer while she takes an eternity to choose an ice-cream. Jake buys her lollies as well. Spearmint leaves. He buys himself overpriced Panadol and a bottle of water.

The park is abandoned. Streaks of white-hot light blaze down the shafts of the metal play equipment.

'Push me on the swing.' La-Li yanks his arm, runs on the spot until he follows.

His hands fit in her armpits as he lifts her into the swing.

She jiggles in the seat. 'It's hot,' she says, lifting one bum cheek and then the other.

'You want to get off?'

She shakes her head, the wispy ends of her pigtails flinging back and forth over her face.

'Okay then, hold on.' Jake steps behind the swing and grips the scorching metal chains. He lifts her high, high as his chin. 'Holding on?'

She nods a single nod. Up and down. Definitive and definite. Like her mother used to do. Probably still does.

He lets go and her giggle spurts over the scorched playground like a sprinkler.

Later, he sits at a table in the shade and watches her pick weedy dandelion flowers from the edge of the playground. She talks to herself, her glossy lips dance over quick quiet words, her tiny head gestures and questions. Her dress pulls up when she bends and reveals Dora on her knickers. Her legs are skinny and pale, unblemished. Her perfection astounds him.

His head still throbs, thump, thump, a mallet banging the blood through his temples. He lays his head on the table. Near his head is a sickly blob of dried tomato sauce. Or blood? He picks at it with his nail. Sauce.

He closes his eyes.

The girl in pink smiles at him. Freckles mess across her nose and across her cheeks.

'Daddy!' Jake wakes with a jolt. La-Li tugs his shirt sleeve. 'Daddy, wake up, I'm hungry.'

He rubs his eyes and they make a gristly sound in his head. His hangover is craving something greasy. Chips. Burger.

'You want to go to Maccas?'

'Yes! Yes!' La-Li bounces and twirls. 'Yes! Yes!'

He stops her with a hand on her shoulder. 'La-Li, look at me.'

She stops bouncing and focuses on his face.

'La-Li, if we go to McDonald's, you can't tell Mummy.'

The ends of her mouth turn down. 'Why?'

'Because it will be our secret.'

She shakes her head. There is still ice-cream chocolate in the corners of her mouth. 'Mummy says I can't keep secrets. Secrets are dangerous. Especially when a man does something and tells you it's a secret.'

'I am not a man. I am your daddy.'

La-Li kicks a tuft of grass. 'Mummy says expecially you. I can't do secrets with you.'

'Especially me?'

'Expecially you.'

Jake scrapes his hand through his hair. 'Well, that's very trusting of the bitch.'

La-Li stares at him, her chin jutted out, pointed.

'Let's get in the car.' He steps over the picnic seat. 'Let's get some saturated fat and salt.'

'Yah! Statuated fat and salt.' La-Li skips ahead him. 'Statuated fat and salt. Statuated fat and salt for me!' she sings.

The toy in the Happy Meal is something from the latest Disney movie. Some sort of creature with fur. Jake doesn't recognise it, but La-Li has seen the movie and recites dialogue while she chews. The pit of hurt in his stomach expands. He misses so much of her life. How can he make up for what he misses in just one Sunday a month?

She wants to play in the restaurant playground, but the boys in there are big and loud and rough. 'Let's go for a walk instead,' he suggests.

Jake takes her to the boardwalk on the river. He strolls while she runs ahead, stands on her tippy toes and peers over the rails into the brown muck of the river. Sweat crawls down his spine.

He catches up to her and they sit side by side, their legs dangling over the edge. 'Careful,' he says.

She nods back at him. 'I know, Daddy.'

He wraps his arm around her shoulder and pulls her close. 'Too hot,' she says and squirms away.

'Right,' he says, the small space between them too wide for him.

They watch the river swirl and twist around rubbish and weeds. 'It looks like chocolate icing,' La-Li says.

'I wouldn't eat it,' he says and tickles her. She giggles and writhes further from him.

Her little feet swing back and forth, the remnants of red nail-polish chipped from her toes. He takes a breath and asks the question he doesn't want to ask. 'Does Mummy have any man visitors?'

'There was a man,' La-Li says. 'I wish the water was clean and we could jump in it and swim and swim and swim.'

'Who was the man?'

'He came and fixed our washing machine and then he came back.' La-Li picks a leaf up off the boardwalk and throws it in the water.

'He came back?'

'The machine broke again! Mummy said he was so useless.'

'Okay, so no special man. You know like a… boyfriend-like man.'

La-Li scrunches her nose. 'Yuck. Mummy doesn't have boyfriends.'

Jake grins and twirls La-Li's pigtail between his fingers.

'There's only Sandy,' La-Li says matter-of-factly.

'Yes, but Sandy's a girl.'

'Aha.' La-Li nods. 'A girlfriend. A special girlfriend.'

'All girls have girlfriends. Don't you have a special girlfriend?'

'Yep.' La-Li turns to face him, her eyes big. 'Caitlin is my special friend, but she's not special like Mum says Sandy is special.'

So, that is the truth of it. He imagines ripping open his chest and tearing out his heart. Chopping it into bits. Handing it to his wife. His ex-wife. 'We have to go.' He stands up. 'I have to get you back by four.'

When they pull up at the house, Carla waits on the top step, her body pulled into a frown. La-Li races to the top, her Disney toy stretched out in front of her.

'Mummy, look what I got…'

She grips La-Li's cheeks in her hands and turns her face left and right.

Jake stops two steps below her.

'She's sunburned!'

Jake's heart sinks. The sunscreen unused, forgotten on the floor of the car.

'I told you to get that step fixed,' he spits back, kicking the loose tread.

'I can't trust you with anything.' She pushes La-Li toward the house. La-Li stumbles on the step. Jake reaches out to catch her. Empty air. Carla tugs La-Li upright. Her tiny feet pushed forward, her body leaning back toward him. Her pink face looks back at him from the doorway. The door slams. He doesn't even get to say goodbye.

He bangs down the stairs and kicks a clump of marigolds out of the ground. Dirt and petals smear over the too long grass. 'Bitch,' he yells at the closed door.

In the car, he heaves out a breath and punches the steering wheel. 'Damn it.' He starts the engine and screams onto the road without looking for traffic.

It's a relief to be on the highway where he can gun the engine, where he can tear along the road. Reckless.

La-Li is the only person in the world I love. The words walk through his mind. A fully formed sentence. He wipes at the wetness collecting in the corner of his eyes.

On the horizon a thunderhead looms, black and fist-like. Tinged with green. Fuckin' hail. He's heading into a hail storm. He turns off the Chilli Peppers and flicks to the radio for a weather warning.

'...Police Service are still seeking urgent public assistance to help locate a five-year-old...' He flicks to another station.

Awful pop music he doesn't recognise. Another station, rubbish country music. He flicks back to the first station. '... severe thunderstorms with damaging winds and hail are forecast for the western districts. People in these areas are urged to secure loose outdoor items and seek shelter indoors.'

He snaps off the radio. The car thrums with silence.

Whatever he has done to La-Li—a little bit of sunburn—she'll live. He's made mistakes. Everyone makes mistakes. Carla, on the other hand... He could never, never, have done what Carla did. All those years ago. Before La-Li. That was no mistake. That was planned. Planned while she left him in the cold with no say. Lightning splits the distant sky. He'll have to stop at Stinky Gully. Seek shelter in the pub until the storm passes.

SUNDAY NIGHT

Bree-Anna needs to pee. She doesn't know where. Which room is the toilet?

She must ask Mr Randall, who she never knew was a stick turned alive. A stick that became an insect that became a monster pretending to be a man.

He made her watch a movie with scary dead shadow mans on horses, and monsters called orcs born in mud, and brave Frodo with big hairy feet. She doesn't know what the movie means. The talking went on a long time, and when the brave Hobbit was in the dark tunnels with the terrible creature, it was too much like Mr Randall, and Bree-Anna covered her eyes with a cushion and pressed her fingers in her ears and could only hear gushing wind in her head. She breathed the plastic smell of Baby and it was enough for her to fall asleep.

But her big-as-balloon bladder woke her. Right away he is beside her. Like he has been watching her, not the movie, which is now a battle of monsters and people and Bree-Anna can't tell which are the goodies and which are the baddies.

'You missed the best bits,' he says. *Scratch, scratch*, he claws his face with his nails, a sound like tree bark.

Bree-Anna lifts herself up to sit, her hair stuck to her face from sweat. She searches for a door that looks like it might go to a toilet. They look like bedrooms, except the one that goes into the kitchen. Her belly is tight like a drum, only an ant would have to step on it and she would burst her pee all over the lounge.

She pulls the elastic of her pants away from her tummy.

The light behind the curtain has less sun. Late in the afternoon she guesses and knows she missed Rachel's party for real, and then there is Rachel's present somewhere out there on the road. Did someone steal it? And Baby's stroller? Mummy will be angry as a brown snake.

She twists her legs, presses them together so the pee won't come out.

'What? What is it?' Mr Randall, the Stick Monster, climbs across the lounge and hangs over her. She doesn't even want to touch where his shadow might be. 'What? What are you doing?'

She swallows and her breath bumps up her body in jumps. 'Toilet,' she says, her mouth almost forgetting how to speak.

'I can't hear you. Talk louder.' He cups his hand around his ear, leans in close, his egg breath in her face.

'Toilet,' she says loudly, almost shouting. Where did her voice find the brave to be so loud? Then she remembers being scared makes you braver and thinks her voice is clever.

The Stick Monster springs off the couch like a jack-in-the-box. 'Of course.' He claps his hands, like he's a little kid. He stops clapping and stares at her like they are about to play a game but she doesn't know what game. 'Go on then.'

'Where?' she asks, her feet on the carpet, her thighs pressed together, knees jiggling, her heels lifting in what Mummy calls her *wanna pee dance*.

'Don't you remember? This way.' And he wiggles his finger

at her and reminds her again of the thing in the dark tunnel with Frodo.

Bree-Anna follows, through the kitchen, dishes and egg cartons all over the place, worse than Mummy when she is feeling lazy, through another door and the bathroom with a toilet in the corner.

Bree-Anna stops, her back to the toilet, bursting, bouncing, dying to go, but he stands there at the door grinning, watching, not going away.

'Go on, go on,' he says, and he steps toward her and she thinks with horror he is going to help her. Pull down her pants like she is a baby and lift her up on the seat. Fast she bends, pulls down her pants. The tight elastic scratches her thighs. She can't think how to hide her bottom from him. The toilet is high, made for giants. She stands on her tippy toes and wriggles up onto the seat. The wee gushes from her and a little bit spills on the seat. Bree-Anna doesn't want him to watch her wiping herself. She slides off the toilet and pulls up her undies and shorts even though it feels yucky and wet.

She turns to flush, but he rushes over. Bree-Anna backs herself against the wall.

'If it's yellow let it mellow, if it's brown flush it down.' And he looks in the toilet as if to check it is yellow. 'Wash your hands, wash your hands,' he says and pushes her to the sink.

Bree-Anna stretches to turn on the tap and he hovers behind her while she washes her hands. She watches him in the mirror, the mirror dirty with toothpaste and spit and black marks that won't ever come off. He grabs her head and turns it from side to side like the hairdresser deciding what to do with Mummy's hair. He bites his lip and looks down to her feet and back up again to her face.

'You're a bit fat,' he says. 'That's okay, isn't it?' Like it is a question he is asking her.

Bree-Anna wipes her wet hands on her shorts. Her voice needs to find some brave again. She swallows and grips the hem of her shorts with her fingers and says, 'I want to go home now.'

'*Nooo*.' His poppy-out eyes pop out more as he shakes his head. 'You have to wait for your mother to come get you.'

She grins, her stomach flips, excited like going down a slippery dip. 'When?'

He shrugs and flicks the hair around her neck. 'How would I know?'

Of course, Mummy will come. He must have rung her while she was asleep. But why hasn't she come already? Is she mad about Baby's stroller and Rachel's present? It wasn't her fault they got left behind. She said to go back, but he didn't go back. It was his fault.

Lightning flashes through the bathroom window.

'Storm coming,' he says and moves his head first to one side, then the other side, so the bones in his neck crack like something broken. *Crack*, *crack*, like a tree splitting in a storm.

Jake shakes the smattering of rain out of his hair. The Stinky Gully pub hasn't changed. It has the ambience of a supermarket. Exactly because it was once a 7-Eleven. So the locals had told Jake when he used to live out here. Small towns, he has noticed, like to recycle buildings: old halls into cafes, banks into art galleries, and coldly lit supermarkets into havens for beer drinkers and poker machine junkies.

He takes his old place at the bar and nods at the barmaid. He recognises her pointy chin and flat chest but can't remember her name. She thankfully seems oblivious to his former tenancy on this particular barstool. It's been a while.

What? Fourteen months, fifteen? Fifteen months since they left Stinky Gully. Fifteen months of him oblivious to the fact that his wife has turned into a muff diver! What does that leave a man thinking of himself?

'A pot of Four-X.' He lays a twenty dollar note on the towelling bar runner.

'Sure,' the barmaid says, spinning the glass around to the tap. Thunder shakes the building. She glances at the flickering lights overhead. 'Gonna hit us good this storm, I reckon.'

'That's what the radio says.' Jake licks his lips. A hair of the dog is what he's needed all day.

She squeezes a phone from her too-tight jeans. She hands Jake his beer and takes his note. 'BOM will tell me,' she says, flicking her finger across the screen. 'Oh yeah, look.' She hands Jake the small screen while she gets his change. A thick band of dark blue and red stretches vertical down the map.

'Coming straight for us. Look, Georgie, this storm coming straight for us.' She takes the phone and walks over to show it to the chick at the other end of the bar. 'Pity that poor kid if she's still out there.'

Jake sighs in relief and sculls half the beer. It fills his parched mouth with yeasty wetness. He wipes his top lip, rubs the bristles on his chin and massages his temples. Tired Christmas decorations wilt from the ceiling.

'It's Jack, isn't it?' A familiar guy plonks himself on the bar stool next to Jake.

'Jake,' he corrects the guy.

'Oh course, Jake. You live up Hill Rise Road. Haven't seen you in a while.'

'Used to live up there, just passing through today.'

The guy pulls his bar stool closer. 'Pete.' He holds out his hand.

Jake shakes it. 'Yeah, yeah, I remember we played some pool together on tournament nights.'

'Pool, that's it! They don't have those tournaments anymore. Hey, Eloise,' he calls down the bar, 'we should have them pool tournaments again.'

'You organise it if you want it,' the barmaid calls back. 'I can't be bothered organising anything for you guys anymore.'

'I'll do that,' Pete calls back and slaps his hand on Jake's shoulder. 'You'll come, won't you, mate?'

Jake shrugs. 'I'm working out at the power station, might not be able to make it.' He looks at his watch. 'I got to get back for the late shift tonight.'

'The power station, hey? Good money?' Pete smooths his handlebar moustache.

'Not bad,' says Jake. A gust of wind shakes the plate glass supermarket windows. A group in their twenties gush through the door, laughing at the weather behind them.

'You should go out to the mines. I heard there's good money working out in the mines.' Pete pushes his empty glass away.

'I need to be close.' Jake finishes the last of his beer and raises his empty glass to Eloise the flat-chested barmaid. 'For my daughter.'

'That's right, you had a little girl. How old is she now?'

'Five going on fifteen.' Jake grins.

'I know what you mean,' Pete says. 'My oldest, Jessica, turned nine last week. She knows everything her old man will never know. Kids are smart these days.'

Jake nods and taps a coin on the bar, hoping to get some attention. 'You were working in the board factory, weren't you, Pete?'

'Yeah, was, then the bastards went into receivership and laid us all off. Still waiting for a payout.'

'I think I heard that,' Jake says.

'I hurt me back.' Pete twists his spine, his palms laid over his lower back. 'I'm lookin' for something a bit softer these days.' He laughs. 'Come on, Eloise,' he calls. 'We're dying of thirst down here.'

Eloise pulls two beers and Jake pays for both.

Pete leans deep into the bar and says in a quiet voice, 'You and your Mrs?'

'Naw,' Jake says.

'That's fucked,' Pete says. 'Sorry to hear that.'

'Yeah, fucked,' Jake says into his beer.

'Hey, you reckon you could put in a word for me at the power station?'

'Don't know.' Jake digs his finger into his temple. 'I'm just casual. My word don't hold too much sway.'

'That's all right, mate, I understand. Just worth askin'. You never know.'

'No harm in asking,' Jake says.

'No harm in askin'.' Pete wipes the condensation off his glass. Rain explodes on the roof. 'Storm's arrived.' He looks at the ceiling.

Someone turns the flat-screen television louder, trying to get above the sound of the rain. Over-excited cricket commentators babble drivel. The twenty-somethings shout over the television noise. Sharp elbows of pain spasm in Jake's head. When Eloise comes to fill his glass, he switches to rum and Coke. Pete disappears before his shout is due, and Jake remembers that was the thing about Pete, there when his glass was empty and gone when it was his shout.

In the alcove off to the left of the bar, the poker machines dance, their lights seductive, like something twirling on a stripper's tits.

'Eloise,' he calls, 'some change for the machines and another rum.'

'Sure thing.' She takes his money. 'Gamble responsibly.'

With the *chunkah* of the fall of each coin into the machine, the pit in his stomach deepens. Responsibility. Who takes responsibility? Jake's been thwarted at every turn. From the first job he had in high school, mowing lawns, that fuck-wit boss accused him of ripping him off. Jake just did too good a job, the tips those housewives gave him were his for the hard work of making sure every nook and crevice of their yards was perfect. They were his to pocket, not his boss's. Some of those women strutted around him in short shorts—on purpose. One even came out to the clothesline in her bra and knickers to get a dress off the line. And they had daughters who watched him through the window. But he never went there. He was there to do a job. He took responsibility for doing a good job and it got him nowhere. It got him sacked.

The machine *click-a-clicks* like long fingernails on a table.

He took responsibility for Carla, for La-Li. He worked all the hours God sent in dead-end jobs to put food on the table, buy a house, have little luxuries.

What a top spin, the machine speaks to him. Like he had any control over it.

Everything he ever did was for her. That bitch says she can't trust him. He gave up everything for her. She took everything from him. The machine *clicks* and *clacks* and Jake presses the buttons—he's not even watching the spins—so when three Aces line up and he wins, the victory music makes him jump. He presses the play button again.

'Another drink, love?' Eloise appears beside him.

'Yeah, thanks.' He drains the last of rum before she arrives with the next. He's pretty sure they're not allowed to do that. That serving drinks in the gaming room encourages irresponsible gambling. He's not going to argue with her.

He never got the car he was saving for with that mowing

job. He gave what he saved to his mother instead. What job did his mum have then? Cleaning at the primary school. She could have gone on sole parent benefits, but she slogged it out in piss poor paying jobs, giving everything to him and his brothers. With a rush he realises he is like his mother. She'd do anything for anyone. Give the shirt off her back to someone she loved and got kicked in the head for it most times. His dead-shit brothers, one still at home, an Xbox zombie growing fat on two-minute noodles, the other stoned much of the time, telling everyone he is writing science-fiction books that are probably not worth wiping your bum on. He's got some kids somewhere he doesn't even bother to try and see. His mother still bailing them out of trouble.

The next big win he'll stop playing and go back to work. But when the Queens line up, he presses play again.

Carla didn't even have the decency to get on with his mother.

And then she goes and shacks up with a woman—leaves him for a woman—a woman who can't even fix the top step of her house. Jake would have had it fixed the day they moved in. There wouldn't be paint peeling from the front door, a gate off its hinges.

Why hadn't he seen it? Back then? All the time Carla and Sandy spent together. That Sandy moved in with Carla when she left him. He must be the dumbest cunt on the planet to let them carry on behind his back.

'Hey, game of pool? We need to make up a foursome.' Pete stands over his shoulder. 'These pokies are for suckers, eat your money. You never win.'

Jake rattles the last of the coins in his cup. 'Whoever expects to win?'

'Team up with me in some pool and we'll win.'

Jake stands and stretches. He glances at his watch. 'I got to get to work by midnight.'

'You ain't going anywhere in this. You seen the weather?'

Jake follows Pete out of the windowless alcove into the bar. On the other side of the glass doors, the wind no longer rages but the rain hammers.

'Rain,' Jake says.

'It's hangin' around,' Pete says.

'Just one game,' Jake says.

'Rack 'em up,' Pete calls over to the table. 'Jack's playing.'

'Just got to get a drink.' Jake turns toward the bar.

'I'll have what you're having,' Pete calls after him.

I bet you will, Jake thinks and orders two rum and Cokes from Eloise.

Jake shakes the hands of the other two men playing pool. Their names fall out of his head as soon as he hears them.

Does Sandy kiss the roses on Carla's back, the way he used to do? Carla had squirmed beneath him then. He thought it was because she wanted him. Was she trying to get away from him? Was it really a squirm of disgust? He helped her choose that tattoo. Her angst over it took so long. She didn't want a tramp stamp. It started with one rose and grew to the Garden of Eden of birds and roses. But it was planned out from the beginning.

'Your shot, Jack,' Pete prods him.

'What are we?' Jake steps away from the wall.

'Big ones,' Pete says.

Jake lines the white with the number ten over the middle pocket.

'I can't understand what she was doing out on her own,' Pete says. 'She's just a little girl.'

They always had good sex after she added to that tat. She

said there was something about the pain. Pleasure and pain, she said.

'She was in my daughter's class,' one of the men says. 'Makes you think.'

'Was?' the other bloke asks.

'They're not going to find her. She's a goner for sure.'

The white ball hits the number ten, sweet, and it sinks into the pocket. Jake rises to survey the table for his next shot. The tat's probably grown since he last saw it. She's probably woven Sandy's name through it. She always refused to put his name on her body. Too tacky, she always said. Too forever is what she meant.

He lines the white with the number twelve. A harder shot, he has to bounce the white off the cushion. He misses.

'There's lots of sickos out there, hey Jack,' Pete says. 'You got to keep your eye on your kids. Can't let them wander the streets. Daughters especially.'

'You do,' Jake says, lifting his rum to his mouth. 'And your wives,' he adds.

They laugh together.

The pub closes at eleven. Jake sits in his car, stale with sweat. The rain has abated to a sleepy drizzle. His brain spins slowly, like a merry-go-round. The rum sits heavy and sweet in his stomach.

Even if he could get to work in two hours, he is too drunk to drive. If he misses his shift, there is no point in turning up again. Ever.

The discarded sunscreen on the floor sets off a wave of fresh guilt. He leans over to pick it up. Beside it lies a white paper bag. He opens the bag, buries his nose in it and smells. Spearmint leaves. He takes one from the bag and drops it in his mouth, the sugar melts, leaving the smooth of the lolly on his tongue. He rolls it over to his molars and chews.

He starts the car, and like a homing pigeon turns left, crosses the highway, past the new supermarket, and takes a right up the hill, toward Hill Rise Road.

Storms scare Baby. Storms used to frighten Bree-Anna too, but since she got Baby and Baby must be cared for, she made herself braver. When it storms, she tells Baby the things Mummy used to tell her. Like: *Only babies are scared of storms.* Or, *Get over it or I will send you out there to see what it is really like.* That hadn't stopped Bree-Anna from being scared. It made her more scared. Then she figured the lightning could find her outside but it couldn't find her inside, so she didn't say her fear, just in case her mother really did make her go outside and see what it was really like.

This night, this storm, she pulls Baby to her hip and says to Baby, in her head with the Magic, *Don't be stupid, the wind won't blow the roof away, even if the house is old. Only dumb-dumbs would think that. Are you a dumb-dumb?* The same thing Mummy said to Bree-Anna one time in a windy storm. 'Dumb-dumb,' Declan had teased her too and Bree-Anna had stopped her talk about the wind. Tonight, it shut Baby up too. She and Baby look at the ceiling every time the wind bangs on the roof and Bree-Anna knows Baby has just pushed the fear down inside.

Mr Randall makes fried eggs for dinner. She sits on the lounge and watches him eat three runny eggs, yellow dripping on his chin. She gags and sips from the can of Coke he's given her. She doesn't like Coke much, but that was all he gave her. Declan loves Coke.

Then Mr Randall says, 'It's almost your bedtime,' and she figures out Mummy must have said her bedtime when he talked to her. Why didn't he tell her that Mummy said she was sleeping the night?

The bed is a hundred high from the floor. A giant bed. Bree-Anna grabs the knobbly brown bedspread to pull herself up, and the cover starts to slide off the bed in her grip. Mr Randall frowns and pulls the bedspread straight again.

'Careful, this is Mother's bed,' he says, and instead of using the ugly bumpy bedspread, Bree-Anna bounces and springs on her feet and jumps up on the bed, belly first and Mr Randall shoves her bum with his hand to get her up all the way.

Bree-Anna scrambles to the top of the bed and jams Baby tight against her.

He sits on the end of the bed and chews, spits a bit of nail on the floor, then jumps up. 'I know what!' He claps his hands together.

From the dressing table he gets a black box with red and gold ladies on it, wipes some dust from the lid and mumbles, then he says aloud, 'Your mother's got dirty sluts doing her cleaning for her. Look...' He holds out his dusty hand. 'See, dust.'

He throws the box on the bed where it bounces and falls on its side. 'The cow she sends now, Eloise... you know Eloise?'

Bree-Anna thinks she knows which one is Eloise, the one they see at the pub when they go there for dinner. She works at the pub at night and is one of Mummy's cleaning girls in the day time.

'Eloise, she got a fat arse like a horse. I like to watch it, blumpa blumpa.' He waves with his hands how Eloise's two cheeks wobble. 'Can't clean for shit though.' He straightens the box and lifts the latch. His stick fingers search through the box and make tinkling and crunchy noises and Bree-Anna guesses there's jewellery in the box.

'I liked it better when your mother did my cleaning. She...' he nods his head at Bree-Anna, 'she takes care of herself. I could wrap me hands around her waist, she's so skinny.' He shows her how skinny with his hands. 'Pity, she ain't taught you thc same. You faaat.' Thunder explodes almost in the room with them and they both jump a little. Mr Randall grunts a laugh. 'That was close.' Then he shakes his head and blinks. 'Nice titties, the size to fit perfect in my hand.' And he holds up his cupped palms for Bree-Anna to see. Bree-Anna covers her chest with Baby and Mr Randall sniggers. 'Your mother, not you. She gonna be well happy when she finds out how good I took care of you. I might deserve a *reward* and I know just what reward I'm gonna ask for.' And his palms feel imaginary titties in the air.

'Meanwhile,' he sighs, and tips the jewellery in the box onto the bed. 'Don't touch, it's valuable.' He holds up a hand like a policeman stopping traffic, though Bree-Anna would never dream of getting close enough to touch.

'This one,' he puts a gold ring on the bed between them, 'was the wedding ring...' He lays down another. 'The engagement ring, and the eternity ring.' Three rings in a row, he considers them a while. 'I had to prise them off the dead bitch myself, else that funeral man would of stole them. Which one do you think your mother would like?'

Bree-Anna's thumb finds her mouth and she sucks it hard.

Mr Randall lays out a row of necklaces, a row of bracelets, and a row of brooches.

'Which one?' he says.

Rain pounds on the roof and explodes against the window. Bree-Anna thinks maybe it could smash the glass.

'Which one?' he asks again, smacking his knuckle on the side of her head. Bree-Anna rubs her temple and sniffs back tears. She takes her thumb out of her mouth and points at the nearest thing, a brooch with a purple stone in the middle and white jewels around it.

'Really?' He rolls the brooch around in his hand and scrunches up his nose. 'It's a bit old-fashioned. Well, if you say so.' And he shoves the brooch into his pocket. 'Here, you can have this one.' He throws her a necklace of shiny blue crystals. She shies from it, like it is poison. 'Take it,' he grinds the words out. 'Take it, put it on.'

She wipes the wet from her eyes, picks it up and wraps it around her neck, fumbles, but can't work the catch.

He tuts, 'Let me,' and standing up behind her, he yanks her hair out of the way and does up the necklace. 'There.' He jerks her around to face him, inspects the necklace at her throat. 'Now you owe me too,' he says with a grin.

Another gust of wind slams at the roof, beating the house with its fists. Thunder thuds on the earth and they both look toward the window.

He shrugs and sits back on the bed. 'I seen some bad storms here, this ain't nothin'. One time a tree, a giant old gum, smashed down on our dairy sheds. Me old man lost the plot, screaming and shouting. God must'a had it in for him. Something the old bastard did.'

He lies down, spreading across the bed. 'We used to own all this land round here, bet you didn't know that, did ya?' He looks up at her. Bree-Anna edges herself away, almost falling off the bed. 'Before all these shiny new houses these bastards come and built, we had all this.' He waves his arms all around. 'Mother sold it to them developers before she kicked the bucket. Didn't trust me to run the place, the bitch.' He yawns and stretches, his T-shirt lifting from his skinny belly, and Bree-Anna wants to tell him to pull up his pants so she can't see the hairy whiteness of him.

'Course,' he goes on, 'now I got all that money. I'm a good

catch. You should tell your mother what a good catch I am. Tell her how rich I am. It's all there in the bank and trusts and shares. I don't know how it works. I pay *the man* to think about that shit.'

He yawns again, though it feels to Bree-Anna like he is pretending, not tired at all, wide awake and rearing to go as Mummy would say.

'It's been a big day,' he says. 'Time for bed.' He twists around to face her. 'You can sleep here,' he pats the bed between them, 'with me.'

She shakes her head no, her thumb popping out. 'Only big ladies sleep in bed with mans,' she says.

'You can't even speak proper,' he says. 'Besides you have to be nice to me or I will tell your mother you were rude. I know your mother doesn't like it when you're rude. What happens when you are rude at home? Huh?'

'I get a smack,' she says under her breath.

'What? Speak up, you gotta learn to speak up,' he shouts, lifts himself up on his elbow and sticks his bony face right up into hers.

She pulls away from his egg breath, makes herself small, Baby tight to her body.

'What the fuck is it with that doll?' he says and snatches Baby from her.

Bree-Anna springs forward, catches only a handful of empty air, Baby's scream in her ears. 'Give her back!'

'What, this?' He holds Baby by a fistful of hair, swings her back and forth. 'This ugly thing.'

Bree-Anna jumps toward him and he throws Baby in the air and catches her. 'Come and get it.' He stands on the bed and Bree-Anna stands on the bed, jumps like it is a trampoline, trying to reach Baby. The jewellery flies everywhere, all over the floor, and Baby crying all the while, *Help me, help me.*

He leaps off the bed, landing on the floor, skipping, and Bree-Anna thinks of Declan and thinks Mr Randall is like a boy. A boy in his head and a man's body to live in. She jumps from the bed, at him, straight at him, but he steps away and she lands on her knees and pain shoots through her.

He spins and spins and squeals and then bends down toward her, Baby held up high behind him. His top lip curls. 'You can't have it.'

He reaches to the top of the wardrobe and takes down a suitcase, clicks it open. Bree-Anna runs at him, screams 'Noooo,' but he grabs her shirt and her skin beneath it and holds her away, his thumb pressing the sharp necklace beads into her throat. He throws Baby into the suitcase and slams the lid. He lets go of Bree-Anna so he can close the latches and she flings herself at him, her fists punching his back. He turns, picks her up, and throws her against the dresser. Bree-Anna bangs her head and her back and the dresser rocks and shakes and the things on it rattle and fall.

He lifts the suitcase back onto the top of the wardrobe.

'Go to bed.' He points at the monster bed, ugly brown bedspread, scattered with what's left of the glittering jewels. The rest of them all over the floor. '*Now.*'

MONDAY MORNING

Jake wakes with the early summer sun. He flicks the ignition key. The clock reads five-fifteen am. He flicks it off, winds down the wet window so he can see outside, and there it is. The house. Number thirty-eight.

When he brought Carla here the first time, she sang the little boxes made of ticky-tacky song.

Was he hurt? He knew she would hate it out here. Her heart was set on an old full-of-character Queenslander in the inner city. He told her this was a stepping stone. They could make money on it and move into a place she liked. It's possible he was punishing her by bringing her here. The truth is he hoped she would grow to like it. The narrow winding roads ending in cul-de-sacs, the new white kerbs, the fake antique looking street lights, the houses popping up every week like mushrooms. These things had filled him with surges of potential and newness. The houses Carla yearned for reminded Jake of the dumps his mother was forced to rent: creaking hot in summer, frigid in winter, deteriorating relics.

He hoped, too, in moments of optimism, that country life would grow on Carla. That she would agree to a few acres.

Land he could build their dream house on. A house they could design together. A house built with his hands, his own thing.

Number thirty-eight needs some care. Weeds line the pebble driveway and the grevilleas he planted have grown straggly and woody. The grass he so carefully tended is thin and patchy with puddles of mud from last night's storm. A string of Christmas lights dangles haphazardly in the conifer, taunting him with their attempt at cheer.

He moves in the seat. He needs a piss. The familiar hangover throb squeezes and releases its grip on his head. The car door screeches open. At the top of the hill, a new street is being born. Like magic. Jake walks toward it, pulling his waistband away from his bloated bladder.

The soft morning caresses him for now; later its sharp tongue will wake to lash the streets with heat and humidity. Behind the security screens, behind the curtains, families will soon stir and give life to the houses made of ticky-tacky.

But the houses aren't all the same, not made of ticky-tacky. Repetition of design is an economic imperative for developers. He learnt that when he did some labouring for a brickie. People transformed them into homes, added gardens, large earth-coloured pots with spiky plants, sandstone mailboxes. The same homeliness he tried to give number thirty-eight. Before Carla wrenched the heart from the hearth.

In the new street, a skeleton of a house stands on damp concrete. Jake takes a piss behind an excavator that curls on the wet ground like a patient dinosaur. Before him, vacant lots stretch along the street. He thinks of them each waiting, ready for a family to stand in the middle of them and imagine a house, imagine a home, imagine a new life.

He should be at work right now. Too bad about that job, it was okay, the boss was okay—and he'd had a shitload of bad bosses. There was the metal polisher who turned the wrong way when they were carrying a truck bull bar. Jake twisted his back to save the bull bar from crashing. It hurt like fuck, he got ice on it right away, and the guy sent him home. Days later it was still up shit creek, and he went to the doctor. The doctor said he should do a worker's comp claim, but when the boss got the claim he lied and said nothing happened at work and Jake must have done it playing football.

That was how he met Carla. She was a friend of the girlfriend of his fullback. Jake played wing. He was fast but frustrated at those greedy front liners. Take the ball up, draw in the defenders. Make a space for the boys with speed and then they don't make the best of it. They all got on a bus together to get to the games, and coming back the beer and Island Cooler would come out. On long trips, they would stop along the way and the boys would all line up along a fence or a building and piss together, thinking about the girls on the bus, and were they watching, and did they fancy them. Carla wouldn't drink the Island Cooler. She said it was too sweet. She drank the boys' beer and when they got back to the pub, she would drink Scotch with ice. She smoked then. Used to blow smoke in the air and hold her cigarette with an angled wrist he found so sexy. She was skinnier then, though never skinny. She always wore short thigh-hugging skirts. The first time he had the guts to touch her he held her bum cheek in his hand and got an instant hard-on. She was smart too. Still is smart. She was at university then. She talked a lot about feminism and women's studies and the history of prostitution and abortion rights and sexual politics. Her confidence with words mesmerised him.

He leans on his wet car and surveys number thirty-eight. La-Li took her first steps in that loungeroom, behind those drawn curtains. He didn't see those first steps. He, as usual, was at work. Carla rang to tell him. La-Li wouldn't repeat the performance when he finally got home. He waited three days for the pleasure of her stumbling toward him, upright and proud of her baby steps.

Jake pulls away from the car, his shirt sticks to his back with wet, he hugs close to the fence, in the long morning shadows. The developers put wooden fences around backyards, seven feet high. Carla called them cages. Jake lifts on his toes and looks through the slats into the backyard. The fort he built La-Li is still in the corner. He spent weeks envisaging, planning, buying the wood, and turning his vision into reality. La-Li spun in circles when he showed her. She fell to the ground giggling. What does Carla say? Is it safe? Is it effing safe! He wanted to slap her.

Kids' bikes and balls litter the yard now. He hopes these new kids like the fort but he wishes it was La-Li hanging off its railings, climbing its ladder. A kookaburra perches on the fence. Its laughter jolts through Jake.

'Yeah, I'm a joke,' he says aloud.

He returns to the car and climbs in the driver's seat. He sits upright, poised to move. He puts the key in the ignition, turns it. He will have to go back to the men's quarters at the power station, show his face, and collect his stuff, such as it is.

He turns the ignition off and falls back into the seat.

In the distance, the highway hums awake. Would La-Li be awake? If he could see La-Li this morning, her tousled hair, sleep in her eyes, clutching whichever stuffed thing was her favourite at the moment. If only he could see La-Li this morning.

Carla's talk of sexual politics and feminism all those years ago got him thinking about his mother. If abortion was easier back in her day, would she have kept him? After all, she'd been shafted by all the men in her life: his elusive father, the dickhead who fathered his brothers. She could have avoided all that.

They were having some drinks one night, for her birthday, when he asked her, 'What would you have been if you could have been anything?'

She'd poured herself another wine and grinned. 'I don't know. The Queen probably.'

'There must have been something,' he persisted.

'I never thought about it much. I wanted to be a nurse once, but I didn't finish school so... it didn't happen.'

'Why didn't you finish school?'

'I was pregnant, you know that.'

'You could have had an abortion.'

She just shrugged.

'You thought about it, didn't you? You would have if you could have.'

'I never regretted having you,' she added.

But the shrug said more. It was the shrug he saw over and over.

That was why he didn't agree with abortion. Terminations, Carla called them. It. She might as easily say friendly fire. It was the same thing.

A sleek jogger passes by his window. Jake sinks down in his seat and closes his eyes. The band of pain tightens across his forehead.

His mother never liked Carla. After La-Li was born, his mother called Carla a breastfeeding Nazi. They fell out the Easter when La-Li turned two. His mother hid Easter eggs throughout the garden, a game she never played when Jake and his brothers were kids. Carla muttered something about too much sugar. His mother gave her a look and Jake, stupidly, changed the subject.

'So, did you see, it's ten years since Kevin Rudd's sorry speech?'

'I don't see why we should say sorry for something we didn't do,' his mother replied.

Carla was quick off the mark. 'So, if someone you know tells you their mother has died, you don't say sorry?'

'Of course, I say sorry,' his mother said.

'But you didn't kill them. You didn't cause their death. You are saying sorry because you are sorry for their loss.'

'I'm not racist,' his mother continued, 'but...'

'But what? Those kids were better off in the long run? It wasn't your generation? It's history and we should just move on?'

'Carla,' Jake tried to interrupt.

'In my experience,' Carla sat upright in her plastic chair, 'when someone says, "I'm not racist but", or "I don't hate gays but", or "I'm not sexist but", they are about to say something racist, homophobic, or sexist.'

'And just how many Aboriginal friends do you have, Carla? What about Alannah, does she have Aboriginal friends?'

'There are Aboriginal people in my office.' Carla sat back in her chair.

His mother stood up. 'Get her out of here, Jake.'

She never went back. Jake thought the Apology was safe ground. He knew his mother was good friends with the old Aboriginal guy down the street. She took him to hospital appointments when his daughters were at work. The daughters came for tea and brought cake to thank her. She always took people at face value. He had never known his mother to judge someone on their race.

Carla accepted La-Li had the right to know her grandmother. To visit her and have a relationship, but she wasn't going to talk to the woman ever again.

A knock on the window startles Jake, and he opens his eyes. A man stands outside the window. Jake winds it down.

'You right, mate?' The man crosses his arms over his chest.

'Yeah, yeah,' Jake says. 'Just waiting for a friend.'

The man leans into the car. 'Maybe you should wait somewhere else.'

Jake turns the key in the ignition and smiles. 'Not a problem.'

The man steps back and Jake pulls away from the kerb. In the rear-view mirror he sees the man standing in the middle of the quiet street—typing, what Jake assumes is his plate number, into his phone.

Bree-Anna lies on her side, balancing on the edge of the mattress like it's a cliff edge, the dark unknown between her and the floor. Better than touching Mr Randall's hairy, skinny, twiggy body, even by accident. Her head aches and tears squeeze out the corner of her eyes. She sniffs and holds her breath, afraid Mr Randall will hear her cry. He starts to snore, and she hiccoughs with tears of relief. Groggy and tired, she wants to sleep, but Mr Randall jerks about and snores and grinds his teeth. *Crunch, crunch, crunch* like a saw. Just as she finally falls asleep, his arm flings out and whacks her in the head. She stiffens, afraid he is awake, but then he snorts and she closes her eyes to force sleep again. She snaps awake just before she falls off the bed. Her heart beats fast. She opens her eyes to darkness. She had dreamt Mummy was not coming because she was mad about the stroller and the present. She got another girl instead. Rachel liked the new girl better too.

She curls her arms around her chest. Just a dream. She strains to hear Baby and thinks she can hear her sobbing and calling. *It's all right, Baby,* she whispers with her Magic, *be brave.* Can she breathe in the suitcase? Is there air? *Sleep, Baby, sleep.*

At last she wakes to grey light, morning shifting into the room. Her tummy rumbles with sick hunger. The last thing she ate was the orange icing biscuits. At the same time, the thought of eating, even the idea of biscuits or lollies, makes her stomach churn and hot vomit taste come up in her throat. Maybe she is getting sick? The last time she was sick was when the troll came into her room. She pushes the sick feeling down, tries not to think about it. Think about Mummy instead. Seeing Mummy and going home.

What time will she come? Bree-Anna thinks she had a bad dream about that; she tries to remember, but it is gone, just the sad feeling the dream left behind. Another thing not to think about. The holidays mean Mummy doesn't have to get up early to get them to school. She likes to sleep in. The pointy necklace digs into her neck. She moves it around to stop the digging. Will he be mad if she takes it off? She dare not move in case she wakes him.

Sometimes Mummy lets Bree-Anna come into bed with her, as long as she is still, doesn't take up too much room, doesn't touch her with cold feet, and doesn't wake her. It is a bit like how she won't touch Mr Randall. She has good practice at being still in bed.

Grandma lets her get in bed with her without any rules. Sometimes when she used to stay at Grandma's house, Mummy would say she was coming one day, but it would be days and days. Her grandma would get angry and shout in the phone and Bree-Anna wouldn't know when she would be picked up. Hopefully it is not like that this time.

Her legs are cramped from not moving. Slow as a snail, she stretches. Lies still and quiet, listening for him.

What if Mummy comes before he wakes? Will she hear her knock on the door? Will that wake him too? How will they get Baby if he is still asleep?

No sound comes from the suitcase high on the wardrobe. Is Baby sleeping? Yes, sleeping. Sleeping peacefully is the best thing to imagine. She should try and get Baby down. So she doesn't wake up and get scared again.

Spread across the bed, Mr Randall snores a horrible snort, and seems to stop breathing before snorting again. Bree-Anna slides, first her legs, very slowly toward the floor still scattered with his precious jewels. The rest of her body follows until she leans against the bed, waiting for another noise. The place where her head rests on the mattress hurts. She fingers the painful spot and finds a small hurting lump. From the dressing table. She wants to tell Baby he hurt her too. He squirms in his sleep and his teeth grate against each other.

By the window, a chair that has a soft seat with flowers painted on it could be high enough, if she stands on it, to reach the top of the wardrobe. It might be hard to get the suitcase down. Especially without making a noise, but she has to try. The space in her arms where Baby should be is empty and she really, really wants to cuddle Baby.

She tip-toes between the necklaces and earrings toward the chair. Birds chatter outside the window and she glances toward the growing light.

She knows where she is!

She presses her face against the cold glass. On either side of the window, trees hang their wet leaves. Between the two trees extends a paddock of long overgrown grass, and on the other side of the paddock is a high wooden fence. Beyond the fence is the 'far' car park that no one uses much, and there, plain as day—Woolworths. She never knew this is where Mr Randall lived. She knows this house, on its own in the paddock surrounded by big trees. The trees have a vine growing in them and she likes its purple flowers. Mummy said it's a weed and will kill the trees eventually. When they go shopping, Bree-Anne looks at this house and thinks it looks lonely.

That must be why they see Mr Randall at the shops all the time. The shops are his neighbours.

This is good. Mummy will be going to the shops, anyway. She goes every day. When she goes to the shops, she can pick her up. It won't be like she is going out of her way at all. Not like when she has to go and get Bree-Anna from Grandma's house. Back when she used to be allowed to visit. Before Mummy and Grandma's fight about the puppy.

So, she won't come until the shops open. That is for sure. Bree-Anna moves from foot to foot. She needs to pee. She glances up at the wardrobe. At the door. At the bed. Mr Randall has rolled on his side, facing away from her.

Her mum will be even madder if she loses Baby as well as the stroller and the present. If she can get Baby, she can go to the toilet and wait on the front stairs. She might even see Mummy's car coming down the road and go out to her. Then she won't have to go out of her way at all.

Bree-Anna bends over the chair and grips the sides of the seat and grunts. Too heavy. She can barely get it off the ground. She tilts it so two legs are off the ground and bumping the chair over the carpet, she drags it along the floor.

'What the fuck!'

She drops the chair and spins toward the bed.

He jumps up on the bed, crouching on his too long legs and arms, his elbows and knees sharp like pointy knives.

'That's my mother's chair.' He jumps off the bed and snatches the chair from the floor and shoves its legs toward her. 'You can't touch it.'

'I…' Bree-Anna crosses her legs and halfway slides down the wall.

'What do you think you are doing?'

Bree-Anna squeezes her eyes and squeezes her legs together, pushes her hands on her wee-wee.

'Ow, ow,' he copies her, only he makes the dance bigger, clutching himself, 'need to use the loo? Well, not until *you* tell me what you're doing sneaking around. Little sneak.'

Bree-Anna jiggles and taps her foot. 'I…' She tries not to, but her eyes look up at the suitcase, just for a second.

'You're not getting that ugly fuckin' doll back so don't even think about it. I hate that fuckin' doll.'

Bree-Anna nods. 'I—I was just looking…' She points at the window.

'Looking for your mummy?' He tilts his head and smiles. 'Ah, that's sweet. Looking for your Mummy's little red car?'

She nods, locking her knees together. The pee prickles at her wee-wee. She jigs and bolts to the door. His long legs put him steps in front of her; his arm swings back and knocks her in the chest. She falls on her backside and swings herself onto her hands and knees, crawling. He leaps to the door and pulls it open.

'Ha ha,' he pretend-laughs, jumps into the hallway, and slams the door closed.

Bree-Anna leaps up and runs for the door. She wraps both hands around the handle and pulls. The door opens a little, but on the other side, he yanks it closed again.

'Pleeease,' she begs and tugs on the handle. He holds tight on the other side. A warm trickle wets her crotch. She stops pulling on the door. 'Please.' She weeps, crossing her legs, hot urine flooding her shorts. She sinks to the carpet, the gush unstoppable.

The damaged marigold has been poked back into the ground, smashed and broken; it won't survive, but someone is hopeful. Jake trudges up the stairs. His head no longer throbs, but floats balloon-like on top of his shoulders. He stops at the top step and kicks the loose tread.

It has been fixed.

Sandy answers the door. 'What do you want?' she says and tightens a daggy old dressing gown across her chest. Jake wonders if she is naked underneath.

She is older than Carla. He's never bothered to notice before, the lines around her mouth and eyes, the grey flecks in her hair.

'I want to see my daughter.'

'She's still in bed.'

'I'll wait then,' he says and sits down in a cane chair on the veranda.

'That's the cat's chair,' Sandy says and closes the door.

A dusty, web-caked wind chime hangs frozen in the breezeless morning. He leans on the table and rubs his temples.

The door creaks open and Carla comes out onto the veranda. She leans on the railing, her arms crossed. 'What's going on, Jake?' Her dishevelled leopard print hair sticks out every which way. She always said she could never do anything with it in the morning.

'How's La-Li?' He rubs his palms together and stares at his hands. 'Is her face all right?'

Carla sighs and drops her hands to her sides. 'She's fine. It's not bad. Shouldn't you be back at work?'

He shrugs.

'Oh, Jake, not again.' She steps forward and sits in the chair on the other side of the table.

'You're just worried about your child support.' He stretches his legs out in front of him and turns his head away from her.

'I can get by without the child support,' she says.

'Why do you take it then?' He turns back to her.

She shakes her head and sighs, her eyes rolling to the ceiling.

He drags his legs back under the chair. 'Can I wait—till La-Li is up? Take her to child care?'

She doesn't answer.

'Please.' He hates to beg, but the need to see La-Li pulls at him like a drug.

'I'll make you a coffee. You look like you need it.' Carla stands and takes a breath as though to say something else, then lets the breath out, empty of words.

'Thanks,' Jake says.

Sandy appears at the door again, fills its frame and glares at Jake. Carla moves to the door and pushes her back inside, following her. She leaves the door open.

There have been lots of jobs. There is no reason for Carla to be surprised he has left another one. He always finds something else.

Carla returns and hands him a coffee. She smells like cigarettes. He holds the coffee between his hands and looks down the grey floor boards, cat fur stuck between the grooves.

'I didn't know you had a cat.'

Carla shrugs and pulls her gown tight across her chest. 'You hungover again?

He grunts. 'You got a fag?'

'I thought you gave up.'

'I thought you gave up,' he replies.

She reaches into the pocket of her gown and takes out a packet of cigarettes. The soft mound of her breast moves behind the deep blue silk. Jake groans and takes the cigarette.

He takes the lighter from her, her fingers brushing his.

Jake draws on the lit cigarette, his body's memory reeling with remembered satisfaction and guilt.

'Daddy! Daddy!' La-Li rushes at him.

Her face is tinged pink, like a pale carnation.

He leaves his coffee on the table and drops to the ground, hugs her close with one arm, holding the cigarette at a distance with the other. Today she smells of shampoo. 'How is your sunburn?'

'Big trouble,' she whispers. 'I have to take resbonsa-ability for my own skin. That's what Mummy says.'

Jake looks over at Carla. She flicks her cigarette over the veranda rail. 'Don't smoke near her,' she says.

He stands, drops his cigarette on the floor and grinds it with his shoe.

'It's stinky,' La-Li says, waving her hand in front of her face.

Sandy hovers near the door, giving them both a filthy look. 'Come and get dressed.' She points a finger at La-Li.

'No!' La-Li crosses her arms over her chest and pushes out her bottom lip so far you could dance on it. That's what his mother always said to him when he pouted.

Carla says, 'Go and get dressed.'

'I want Daddy.' She grips his leg.

Carla holds her daughter's gaze. 'Alannah-Lily, go and get ready. Now.'

La-Li relinquishes possession of his leg and stomps across the veranda, throwing one last defiant look at her mother as she disappears into the house.

Jake breathes in a ragged breath and fights the barb of tears.

'You coulda let her stay.'

'You could have let me know you were coming.'

'It was spur of the moment.'

'It always is with you. What happened to going back to work?'

'I got stuck in Stinky Gully.' He hopes the name of the town will spur some guilt in her. 'The storm.'

Carla huffs. 'Might have known. How is the Stinky Gully pub? Fucking Stinky Gully,' she says with gusto. 'We never should have gone there. I hated that town.'

'It would have been a safe place to raise La-Li, better than here.' He swivels his head to indicate the general decay he sees.

'Haven't you been listening to the news?' Carla replies.

She pulls at her pocket for the cigarette packet. Her gown parts and he glances a flash of white underwear. Heat fills him.

'What's with Sandy? You a couple?'

Carla nods slightly.

'Why didn't you tell me?' He exhales, picks up his coffee, hoping to still the wobble in his breath.

'I thought you knew.'

'Thought I knew!' He thumps his hand on the arm rest. His coffee wobbles and splashes on the ground.

'Keep your voice down,' Carla says in a low voice.

'It makes sense now.' He stands and leans into her face, saliva spitting over his lips. 'Why you left. I thought it must be another man... but I couldn't see a man. Only Sandy. Good old Sandy.'

Carla meets his gaze, rigid and cold.

'So you like girls now? Did you always like girls? Was I just a consolation prize?'

'It's none of your business, Jake.' She pulls hard on her cigarette and the lines around her mouth pucker like an arse.

'Fuck you.' He turns and kicks the chair. The coffee still in his hand spills out over his arm. 'Damn it.' He scowls at her, puts the coffee cup on the table, and flicks the liquid from his skin.

'Daddy.' La-Li walks onto the veranda, a daring look at her mother. 'Brush my hair. Put it in a ponytail—like this.' She turns her back to him and holds her hair high up on her head.

Carla rips the brush from her hand. 'Sandy will do it. Daddy is leaving.'

Thunder surges through Jake. His fists coil into tight knots.

Spread Carla's face with his knuckles. Pummel her. He turns, grips the table, grunts with animal ferocity and slams it to the floor, where it crashes and splits, the coffee cup splinters. He twists toward Carla.

La-Li clutches her mother, her carnation face hiding in her mother's dressing gown. Carla pulls her closer and shakes her head at him.

'Get out of my house!' Sandy looms over him, a telephone raised above her head like a weapon. 'I'll call the police.'

'Don't worry, I'm going.' He pushes Sandy aside, his gaze still on Carla.

Halfway down the stairs, he hears the sniff of La-Li's tears and regret descends on him like a collapsing wall.

'Get your life together, Jake,' Carla shouts at his back.

A bit rich coming from the person who ripped his life apart, but he can't find the energy to shout back at her.

MONDAY LUNCH

Bree-Anna stands on tiptoes, her nose pushed against the window, her breath fogging the glass. Below her the garden tangles, a mess of weeds and long grass, like a garden made special for hide and seek. The windows in her house slide open. She thinks this window lifts but she can't get it to work. She pushes up, but her hands slide on the glass now grubby with sweat from her palms.

The door wouldn't open either. She tried to open it after she wet her pants. She rattled and rattled it, but it is stuck. Stuck, stuck, stuck. She is stuck.

She doesn't take her eyes off the shopping centre car park. She watches every car driving down the road. A little red car comes, a bit like her mother's, and her heart beats fast. She watches it turn into a car space. Waits and watches, hopeful, excited, but even though the people who get out of the car are far away and small, she can tell they aren't her mother or her brother. She recognises other cars. Her teacher, Miss Beamer, parks close to the fence and gets out wearing shorts. She's never seen Miss Beamer in shorts before. Just the skirts and shirts she wears on school days. She sees her neighbour too, but she doesn't know his name. They wouldn't hear her if she yelled out. It is too far. Only Mr Randall would hear her.

The TV in the other room blasts like a loud speaker. She hears his footsteps outside the door and claws dig into her back and she feels sick. He walks past the room, but the shivers don't go away.

Her shorts and undies have dried uncomfortable and stiff. She walks like a cowboy, her legs wide apart. It would be best if Mummy goes to the shops and *then* comes and gets her because she can't go to the shops with wee-wee pants. Declan—she wishes Declan doesn't come at all. Mummy will be mad but Declan will tease her forever and ever if he knows she wet in her pants. Even if it was Mr Randall's fault.

Her tummy churns with the hungry sick from when she woke up.

Imagine if her mother makes her go to the shops and Rachel sees her with pee pants. Rachel will never be her friend again. Rachel will be best friends with Tegan instead. Tegan always tries to push Bree-Anna out of the way so she can have Rachel to herself. Tegan would have been at the party. What happens if they don't get Rachel's present back? Rachel will think Bree-Anna is a bad friend if she doesn't give her a birthday present.

She made such a mess when she got into Mr Randall's car. She always makes messes. She cleaned up all the necklaces and brooches and put them on top of the dresser. So there is that, one less mess. There's wee on the carpet still but she can't think how she would clean that. It will have to dry in the air. It will still be stinky, she thinks. How would Mummy's cleaners clean wee off carpet? How would Eloise do it? Would Mummy make a person pay more for a job like that?

She made a mess of Mummy's computer the other week too. Things got missing somehow, important things. Her mother said, 'I don't know why I ever had you. I should have got rid of you while I had the chance.'

What chance? Bree-Anna wanted to ask. *When?*

Was her getting into Mr Randall's car another chance for Mummy to get rid of her? Like a second chance?

Another red car comes around the corner and Bree-Anna lifts higher on her toes and presses her nose hard so it squashes on the window. But the car is the wrong shape. Too round, not long at the front like their car.

Then, of all things, she sees Mr Randall's froggy green car go in the car park. Her arms and legs relax with relief. He won't be coming in the room any time soon. She pulls away from the window and her breath leaves another foggy circle on the glass. She creeps to the door. She doesn't know why she creeps. It is like when she and Rachel tell secrets to each other in whispers even though no one is around to hear them. The TV has gone quiet too. She turns the doorknob. Grandma has olden-day metal knobs like these in her house. Usually you just turn them, but sometimes, like the door that goes to the spare room, the door sticks, like it is crooked in the wall. Grandma told her to wiggle it and pull it at the same time. She turns the knob, she wiggles and pulls, but the door stays stuck. Then thinking maybe, she is going the wrong way, she wiggles and pushes. She barges it with her shoulder. Nothing. Stuck like glue. She drops to the ground and leans against the door. Shifts away from the damp patch of her wee on the carpet. She touches the lump on the back of her head.

'Mummy, hurry up. I don't like it here,' she says aloud, though Mummy can never hear her.

She drags her knees up to her body and her head falls on them. She cries, her body shudders, her thumb not good enough to even bother with. *Baby*, she pleads. Baby doesn't answer.

Poor Baby, scared Baby. Bree-Anna pulls herself up. Still hiccoughing with sobs, she drags the heavy flower chair over to the wardrobe. Stretching, her fingers reach and wiggle. She can barely brush the top of the wardrobe, let alone reach the handle of the suitcase. She drops back down into the seat.

'Sorry, Baby,' she whispers. 'You'll have to wait for Mummy.'

She tugs the chair back. Little dents in the carpet show where the chair lives and she hopes, is pretty sure, he won't know she moved it.

At the window, she checks for changes in the car park. The froggy car stands out like a sore thumb, as Grandma would say. She can't see Mummy's car. She checks around the car park three times to make sure, though there are some cars she can't really see properly. She might be there.

They often see Mummy's clients at the shops. Most of them are ladies with children, and sometimes Bree-Anna knows the kids from school. They always have to say hello Mrs Whoever and be polite, because it is 'good for business'. The ladies always rush off with something to do and somewhere to be. They say hello to Mr Randall, but he never talks back; he looks at the floor and frowns so Bree-Anna thinks he wants to poo and can't. He sits around a lot, on the concrete seats near the newsagent, or by the cheap shop. She's seen him get in his froggy car too but never thought much about him.

There was one day though, while she waited outside the newsagent for Mummy to buy envelopes and pens, he came and gave her a packet of snakes. She said thank you Mr… but that day she couldn't remember his name. She's got better at names since then. She hid the lollies in her shirt, but her mum saw them when she got in the car.

She'd said, 'Where'd you get those? Did you steal them?'

Bree-Anna said no, she would never steal anything, ever. Except maybe a flower from a garden, but she didn't say that.

'Where then?' her mother demanded.

'I got them from a Mr.'

'Mr? Mr who?'

'Mr who you clean for.'

'Don't take lollies from people.' She made Bree-Anna hand them over.

Later, when they sat down to watch a movie, the lollies appeared. Mummy ate them too. Declan pigged out on big handfuls. It wasn't fair because they were her snakes.

Was taking lollies from people the same as getting a lift with them? Is that why Mummy was mad and didn't come?

'What I need to do,' she whispers up to Baby in the suitcase, 'is talk to Mummy on the phone.' Tell her where the stroller is and where Rachel's present is and tell her she is sorry for getting a lift with Mr Randall.

'I don't think he ever was going to take us to the party,' she says. Silent Baby. 'Don't be mad, Baby, I didn't mean it. It was an accident.'

She peers out the window and tries to figure out how far it is to the ground. Far way. The house is tall, with an underneath you can walk through without bumping your head. Even tall people.

Somehow, she misses the froggy car leaving the car park. A rattle at the door sends a rush of blood through her body and she tingles all over. She puts her back to the window and wraps her arms around herself, like a hug.

He comes into the room and holds plastic bags up high with a big grin on his face. 'Presents!' From a bag he gets a nightie, pink with pictures of pussy cats. The smile is gone from his face. He throws the nightie at her face. 'Get changed, stinky pants.'

She lets the nightie fall to the ground at her feet. It's not night time, she thinks. Is taking lollies from people the same as taking a nightie? It seems worse—you can eat the lollies and they are gone, but a nightie is always there. Like the necklace he made her take.

'Fuckin' put it on. I can't have you in here smelling like a piss bucket.'

She bends and picks up the nightie, touches the end of her t-shirt, fiddles with the ends, lifts it to her belly button and stops, watching him.

He grunts. 'As if I want to see what you got, fatty pig. Hurry up, or I won't show you what else I bought.'

She pulls off her T-shirt, his eyes on her.

'I been thinkin' we need to get our story straight,' he says. 'What we'll say is I found you wandering around in the bush.'

Bree-Anna quickly shoves the nightie on her head and struggles to find the arm holes. She twists in a panic, hoping he can't see *what she has.*

'Like, maybe,' he continues, 'the bush at the back of the school. I can say I was... I don't know, maybe I had a dream that was where you were, like one of them psychics.'

She finds the armholes and yanks the nightie over her body.

'Your mother will be on her knees when she finds out I rescued you from certain death in the wilderness. Well,' he laughs, 'while she's down there,' and he thrust his hips at her, grinning with little teeth.

Bree-Anna puts her hands under the nightie and wriggles, struggling to pull down her shorts and knickers that have stuck to her body.

'You can tell her what a good catch I am. About all my money. Remember I said about my money? We can go to dinner. At the pub.' He looks at her, his finger on his lips. 'Oh, I guess you can come. We should go back to your place, or my place.' He looks around. 'Messy bitch doesn't clean properly. We'll go to your mum's place.' He sits on the bed.

'I bet she's hot in bed, your mum. I could show her a thing or two,' he says and takes the brooch from last night out of his pocket and turns it over and over.

Bree-Anna stands, her dirty clothes in her hand. She holds them up.

'Ahh, yuck, throw them out the door.'

Bree-Anna throws the clothes through the doorway.

'That's better, now look.' He opens another bag and licks his lips.

Bree-Anna's heart sinks. Lollies. Lots of lollies. And Fanta. Her belly is too sick for lollies and soft drink.

'Remember when I got you those lollies that other time?'

'Snakes,' she says.

'Eat them.' He throws her a mixed bag. 'That bag's got teeth in it, and raspberries. Did you like those other lollies I got you that day?'

She nods.

'Did you share them?'

She nods again.

'Good girl. Open those.'

Bree-Anna rips the packet with her teeth and he snatches it from her and searches through it. 'You know, your mother should never have let you wander around on your own. Lucky I picked you up 'cause your mum knows me.' He stretches a red snake out with his teeth. 'She likes me. Come and sit on the bed.' He pats the bed beside him.

She springs up onto the bed. It is getting easier.

He shoves the packet back at her. Bree-Anna's stomach squeezes sick at the sight of the coloured sweet lollies. She thinks she would like toast. Just toast and Vegemite. But she doesn't want to ask.

'What I am wondering is,' he grins, red snake caught and chewed up in his mouth, 'why hasn't your mother come and got you? What do you think?' He cocks his head on the side.

'I think she's mad at me,' Bree-Anna says, her hand hovering near her mouth. She wants to suck her thumb but doesn't.

'Mad at you! But why? Because you're fat?'

Hot tears collect in Bree-Anna's eyes. 'Maybe,' she says, suddenly believing it.

'Mmm,' he replies, tipping a handful of lollies in his hand and shovelling them into his mouth.

Be brave. Ask. The more scared you are the *harder* it is to be brave. She never knew. Grandma lied to her. She has been lying to Baby. But she must ask. She takes a deep breath. 'Can we ring Mummy?'

He chews on the lollies, his mouth wide open, the colours mixing into a gooey mess. Bree-Anna's stomach stirs sicker. At last, he swallows with a thick gulp. Then he hangs over the edge of the bed and searches beneath it. He pulls out a tin pot with handles. 'See this? Know what this is?'

She shakes her head.

'It's a chamber pot, stupid. You don't even know what it is for, do you? Stupid. It's for peeing in.' He throws the pot at her.

The pot hits her elbow with a clunk and clatters onto the floor. Bree-Anna rubs her elbow.

'Use it,' he says and gathers up the lollies, 'and drink this.' He points to the soft-drink. 'We don't want you getting dehydrated.' He walks out of the room.

She hears him this time, turning a key in the lock. The door is not stuck, it is locked. Why would he lock the door?

The TV snaps on again and Bree-Anna returns to looking out the window. The car park is busy with huge trolleys of Christmas food. Mummy always parks close to the doors. She says she doesn't believe in walking more than she has to. But the car park is so full today she might have to park near the fence side. Closer to the house. She will complain about how far she has to walk in the hot car park. Bree-Anna can wave and her mum might see her. If she looks over at the house.

Maybe, she thinks, it is not as bad as her mum getting rid of her. Maybe it is more like the times when Mummy won't talk to her. Like when she broke her Mummy's phone, the one before the one she has now. Bree-Anna dropped it and the glass cracked. She didn't mean to—it was an accident. She wasn't supposed to play with it, but sometimes she was allowed to play with it, and it was difficult to know when she was allowed and when she wasn't.

Her mum didn't talk to her all through the rest of the day, all through dinner, even though Bree-Anna said so many times that she was sorry, but her mum wouldn't look at her, wouldn't say goodnight when Bree-Anna came in special to say goodnight. Bree-Anna tossed and turned in her bed, she couldn't sleep. How to show her that she was sorry? How to get her to forgive her? The next morning her mum stayed in bed late and Bree-Anna and Declan got ready and went to school on their own. When they got home that afternoon, everything was normal again and her mum had a new phone that was 'even better' than the old one. There were other times her mother stopped talking to her, but that was the longest time.

Maybe this was just like that? Her mum was doing her silent not talking to her thing. Her mother would like her again soon. Then she would come get her.

Her legs ache, sweat wets the back of the nightie that is starting to feel too small and tight. She sits on the floor to rest. Just for a little while.

What if Mummy doesn't come? Who else would come and get her? Grandma would come. But Mummy won't talk to her anymore. That was Bree-Anna's fault too, another mess she made. So, Grandma won't know she is here. Who would tell her? No one. Rachel can't come on her own, and she is probably angry about the party, anyway.

Her dad might come, if he knew she was born. Maybe he does know she is born! Hades is not the hot bad place her mother says it is. Hades is an island in the sea and her dad is the prince of the island. His father, the king, wants him to marry a princess from another island and wouldn't let him marry Mummy. But he thinks about her all the time. She imagines him; he's tall and he has brown curly hair. He wears gold rings on his fingers and one of them, on his little finger, is the ring he wanted to give to Mummy, but before he could, his father, the king, had his soldiers snatch away the prince and bring him back to the island. The king has banned all the boat drivers from taking her father to see her mother. They don't have telephones on the island because it is too far away.

But one day he gets a letter. A secret letter from Mummy's fairy godmother. It is magicked so the only person who can see it is the prince. It tells the prince that Bree-Anna has been borned and kidnapped. The prince doesn't know what to do. He begs the king to let him rescue her, but the king won't let him. The king won't talk to him and goes to bed without talking to the prince ever again.

The prince gets all the money and jewels in the king's safe and takes it to a boat driver and pays him to take him to Stinky Gully. There is no ocean in Stinky Gully, but he will get to the nearest place. That was last night. He has to get here, but first he has to fight the soldiers who have been sent to catch him. He will turn up soon.

Then he can give the gold ring to her mother and they can all live together.

Mummy wouldn't get headaches anymore. She won't get

mad at Bree-Anna ever again. She will let Bree-Anna snuggle in her bed every morning. Declan can have the prince as a daddy, even though he has a different father, really. His really dad is dead so he won't know.

Kidnapped? Is she really? No, kidnapped would mean she is here in secret. Mummy just hasn't come and got her yet. Mr Randall said she was coming. Why do they need a story about him finding her in the bush?

Her father might really be a policeman or a fireman. He will come with a big ladder and open the window and carry her down.

Grandma will find out she is here. Declan will ring and tell her. She will come straight away. Even if her chickens need feeding or her dogs need walking, or a cat is having kittens, Declan will tell her on the phone and she will drop everything and come and get her.

She stands up again and stares out the window. A fairy floats past the window. The seed twirls and turns on the other side of the glass, fluffy and white. She wants to catch it, make a wish. Just like they do at school. The kids chase them all over the oval. They try to catch the ones you already wished on so they can steal your wishes. Rachel calls them Santa Claus and says they take Christmas wishes to the North Pole. It is only three sleeps till Christmas, but Bree-Anna doesn't want to wish for any presents.

She doesn't care if there are no presents for her under the tree at all. Ever. She would give up all her presents for someone to come and get her right now, this very second.

Eloise's shift at the pub last night finished late. Most run-of-the-mill Sundays finish early, but the full-on storm that came over kept people indoors and drinking. Sent them kind of hypo. An old face turned up. Jake. It took her a while to remember who he was, but then it clicked. He left town a year or so ago. His wife left him for a woman. That's what Eloise reckons, anyway. She has no proof, but she saw the two women together a couple of times and got that feeling there was more going on than just friends. And, when she ups and leaves Jake, she goes and lives with this same chick. So, Eloise figures one and one makes two.

Jake had moped about the bar, the pokies, and the pool table. Still not over it apparently. Pity, he was a nice guy. She'd take him home. If she were that sort of woman. But she wasn't. It wouldn't surprise her if Amber had, but who knows. She's not sure they even know each other.

Eloise drags herself out of bed and shuffles through the tick-tock-clock too-quiet house.

'Mum, Dad,' she calls, snapping the jug on to boil.

She wanders outside, past her mother's heat-withered annuals, and checks the garage. The car's gone. Thank god, she'll have some time to herself. Inside she turns Triple J up high, the air-con on blast, and with the first sip of coffee, sighs at the small joy it brings.

She's got a double shift at the pub today, but no cleaning jobs. First, she must visit Amber. She does not want to visit Amber. Visiting Amber is the right thing to do. God damn Amber; trust her to let something like this happen to her.

She flicks through Facebook while she drinks her coffee and there she is shared over and over. Bree-Anna. Missing. Poor kid. Fat and stupid, but she didn't deserve a neglectful slut for a mother. Who lets her little kid walk off down the highway on their own? Eloise shares the post, not sure what it will achieve. Surely everyone has seen it already. Besides, no one thinks the kid's still alive. Some sick bastard has had his way with her and thrown her in the river, or buried her in his backyard. You don't think things like that will happen in Stinky Gully.

True, the town has changed since all those new developments and new people came, so who knows what nutters might have moved in. That old Randall woman selling all her farm land was the worst thing that ever happened to Stinky Gully. Not that Colin was capable of running the farm. A few sandwiches short of a picnic. 'Abortion', they called him when they were all at high school. A mean nickname, but he was a waste of good air that someone else could be breathing.

And she had to go clean his house tomorrow. What sort of waste of breath did that make her?

She tips the last of the coffee down the sink. She could have gone into town to pick up her prints, but she'll visit Amber instead. Best Amber sees her as 'there for her'. There could be more work in it. Something better than cleaning even.

She showers and dresses in her pub clothes, jeans and the polo shirt with Stinky Gully Pub printed over her weeny pathetic breasts. There was a guy last week, looked her up and down and said, *Look at those tits,* as if to say, you ain't got nothin' love, why do you even bother? She tried once to draw Mike into a conversation, did he like them, were they good enough? But he didn't bite. Mike's wife has good tits. She's only laid eyes on her twice, but she's gotta be at least a double D. Maybe Mike wasn't a boob man. Well, she grunts to herself, maybe he was a bum man. She had plenty of that goin' on.

The bedroom swelters, and she's sweating already. Another stinking shit day. She douses herself in more deodorant, grabs her handbag and keys, and in the loungeroom stands with her face under the air-con to blow the sweat away before she ventures into the heat. She shakes the front of her shirt to chase the cool air down. She's still got two photos to take for her portfolio. When is she going to find the time for that? Who is she going to use? Taking photos of people is the hardest. Character portraits! The landscapes and still-lifes are hopefully strong enough to overlook the shit she'll have to put in for the portraits.

She turns and lifts her shirt, and the cold air slides over her back. She's procrastinating. Should she take something to Amber? Flowers? Food? What do you take a woman who's lost her kid? Disappeared to no one knows where. Her camera? Portrait of a woman grieving! Maybe not. Her mother would call that inappropriate. It's all right when a journalist does it, but not one of your employees, even if you did go to school with them and you have known each other since you were four years old.

The phone rings. She glances at the number on the caller ID, but doesn't recognise it. She turns the radio down and at the same time hears a car in the driveway. She peeks through the window. Her parents are home. She clicks off the air-con, the phone ringing in her hand. It drives her father batty—wasting electricity. Power bills climbing sky high. All the government's fault, apparently.

She presses the talk button. 'Hello?'

'Eloise?'

Her breath leaves her. 'Anthony? Where are you?' she whispers into the phone. Splits the curtain. Her mum and dad pull into the garage.

'Sydney, still.'

'Right. How's it going?' Loaded question.

'I'm clean,' he says. 'Been clean for six months.'

'Really?' She drops the curtain as her parents appear through the garage door. She heads down the hall to her room.

'Really, truly.'

'Ah huh, that's good,' she says, closing the door behind her.

'Is Mum there? Or Dad?'

'Um.' She sits on the bed and twists her arm under her elbow. 'No, they're out.'

'Where?'

'Where? How should I know? I'm not their keeper. They were gone when I got up.'

'You're whispering like they're there.'

'No, I'm not,' she says louder.

He doesn't reply. She untwists her arms and plants her feet firm on the floor. 'What do you want?'

'Just wanted to see how everyone is. Mum? Dad? You?'

She shrugs. He can't hear her shrug, but she shrugs anyhow.

'Eloise?'

'Mum and Dad are good. We're all good.' Lies, but he's no help so what's the point of the truth.

'I thought I might come up for Christmas. You know, catch up properly.'

'That's like what'—she counts in her head—'in three days.'

'Yeah, I know.' He laughs, and his laugh hasn't changed, the same cheeky joyous laugh, and she wants to reach across the state border and slap him. 'I left it to the last minute.' The laughter leaves his voice. 'I just wasn't...'

Straight enough to know what day of the week it was? But she doesn't say that. She says, 'What day are you arriving? Are you flying? Or busing it?'

'Well...'

Silence ticks down the phone line.

'Well?' she asks, but she knows what's coming.

'I don't have any money.'

'Of course, you don't.' She stands and paces the short edge of her bed. 'Cause you shot it all up.'

'I said I was clean.'

'Yeah, right. You know last time Dad sent you money.

Remember that? You know where that money came from?' She paces, realises her voice is rising and brings it back down. 'Mum sold that antique sideboard. The one that belonged to her mother. She *loved* that sideboard. How high did you get off that sideboard? You think Mum and Dad are made of money? They can barely pay the electricity bill. I don't know what they're gonna do when I leave next year.'

'Where are you going?' he interjects.

'There is no way we are sending you a cent.'

She flops on the bed. Grits her teeth. She can hear his breathing, heavy on the other end of the line. 'I just want to come up for Christmas,' he says at last. The words shake, and she thinks he might be crying.

'Anthony,' she sighs, 'I just...'

'I know,' he says. 'I... fucked up big. But I'm for real this time. I promise. Think about it. Please.'

There's a knock on her bedroom door. 'I gotta go,' she says. 'I got a double shift.'

'I'll ring back.'

'No! I'll ring you.'

'The number...'

'Yeah, yeah, it's on the caller ID. Don't ring here,' she says and hangs up.

She opens the door to her mother bending into it, ready to knock again.

'Who are you talking to?'

'No one.' Eloise pushes through the door. 'I gotta go. I got a double shift and I want to visit Amber on the way.'

'Oh, poor Amber. Give her our love,' her mother says, following her down the hall.

'Eloise,' her father barks, 'you had this air-con on?'

'No, Dad.' She drops the phone back in its cradle. 'I'm going to be late.'

'Well, so long as you're out of bed. I thought you might be still in bed. Have you eaten?' her mother says and plods toward the kitchen.

'I'll grab something at work.' Eloise picks up her handbag. 'I won't be home for dinner either. Double shift.'

Neither of her parents acknowledges her. 'Mum.' She follows her mother into the kitchen. 'Don't cook me dinner, all right?'

'All right.' Her mother turns toward her, looking teary. Eloise doesn't have time for this.

'I'll probably see you tomorrow, okay?'

'Okay,' her mother says. 'Give my love to Amber.'

'I will,' Eloise says, halfway out the door.

Bree-Anna falls asleep at the window, curled in a ball on the floor, her thumb in her mouth, a space in the crook of her arm where Baby would be, should be. She dreams of a prince on the ocean sailing to marry her. She can see the ocean from the window and watches for his boat. She is so happy. Then a storm comes and the waves get bigger and bigger. As big as the house, as big as the sky, higher than the sun. A hand shakes her awake.

'Lunch.' He stoops over her, then drops the white paper parcel on the floor. 'That checkout chick in the take-away, she wants me. Open it.' Huge circles of sweat wet his T-shirt around the armpits. 'Hot out there,' he says, swishing the shirt away from his body.

Bree-Anna uncoils from her sleeping position and opens the paper wrap.

'She's not my type,' he says. 'Got too much tits, but I'd do her.'

Steam from hot chips swirls from within the wrapping. Bree-Anna gags.

'I should have told her I'd do her anyway. She could come around and I'd do her good.' He closes his eyes and rocks his hips back and forth. 'Oh yeah, oh yeah.' He opens his eyes. 'What you looking at, pervert?'

Bree-Anna looks away from him and shakes her head. 'Nothing.'

'Don't tell your mum about her—the checkout chick.' He sits cross-legged across from her. 'I don't want your mum getting jealous of that checkout chick. She means nothing to me.'

'I won't,' Bree-Anna says.

'You want me too. I can tell by the way you look at me.' He leans forward and touches her arm, his knuckles knobbly. Bree-Anna wants to pull her arm away, but it freezes beneath his hand.

'Those big eyes not blinking, all coy like butter wouldn't melt in your mouth. Here.' He picks up a chip. 'Open your mouth.'

Bree-Anna opens her mouth, and he puts the chip in.

'Chew it,' he says. 'You should chew your food forty-eight times before you swallow it.'

Bree-Anna forces herself to chew the mushy chip in her mouth, the feeling like vomit in her stomach. She covers her mouth and gags before she swallows. She takes a deep breath, glances at the suitcase on the wardrobe.

He follows her gaze to the top of the wardrobe. 'My mother never loved me either,' he says. 'Cold as a block of ice. Heart made of rocks. Mean as a buzzing old fly. You know why she didn't like me?'

Bree-Anna shakes her head.

'Eat,' he says. 'Are you on a diet? I didn't mean to say you were fat. It might be baby fat. My mother'—he shoves chips in his mouth and chews and talks at the same time—'hated me because she couldn't get away from my dad because I was born.' Bits of chewed up chip fly out of his mouth. 'She didn't know I heard her say that. She told it to her sister in Sydney. Slut sister. They're all sluts in Sydney.' He stops chewing and stares blankly at the wall. 'I should move to Sydney.' His eyes return to her. 'Anyway, I was one of them late-in-life babies. You know what that means?'

She shakes her head. Her thumb goes in her mouth.

'It's when old people that got no business fucking still go at it and have a baby. How old do you think I am?'

She shakes her head.

'Go on, guess.' He turns his head from side to side so she can have a good look.

She takes out her thumb. 'Fifty,' she whispers.

'Fifty! Fuck you. I'm twenty-eight. In the prime of my life. My sexual peak. Fucking fifty.' He takes a handful of chips. 'You need glasses, dumb bitch.'

Bree-Anna pulls her knees up to her chest and puts her thumb back in.

He stuffs more chips in his mouth.

'Here, I'll show you.' He wipes his hands on his pants and leans over and pulls an old tin box out from under the bed. He opens it and flicks through layers of photos until he finds the one he wants. He holds up a picture for her to see.

'Don't touch it,' he says. 'The baby is me. The one holding me is my sister. Aileen. She's sixteen in this picture.' He turns it around to face him. 'She was pretty.' He flips it back around to Bree-Anna. 'Wasn't she?' He thrusts the picture closer to her face. 'Wasn't she?'

Bree-Anna nods.

'Yeah well, she's not pretty anymore. Gone to pot. Went and

married the first bastard that came along and left me here with the other cold bitch.' He points to the other woman. 'Mottth-her,' he draws out the word and laughs. 'The other one is my father.' He throws the photo back in the box. 'Now you know all about me.'

He eats the rest of the chips. Bree-Anna sips on the can of Fanta he bought her. A ball of sick bubbles up and down her throat.

'Anyway,' he says, scrunching up the paper and throwing it against the dressing table, still a mess with fallen over things and jewels. 'I got something to show you.' He drags a plastic bag closer. 'I went and got some scratchies and look what I saw.' He holds up a newspaper. 'That's you, isn't it?'

It is. A picture of Bree-Anna, on the front page of the newspaper, from the day they had photos at school.

'Read it to me.' He pushes it toward her.

What is her picture in the paper for? Her heart beats fast, her stomach whizzes. Bree-Anna can recognise her name and a number that is her age, and the words Stinky Gully.

'Read it,' he says, teeth together.

'It's too hard,' she says, touching the black-and-white picture of herself. All the girls came to prep on photo day with their hair done pretty, but she forgot it was photo day. A bit of hair sticks out funny from her head.

He rips the paper from her. 'Don't you go to school?' he says.

She nods. Just prep, she wants to say but can't.

'Your mother put this photo in the paper. Dumb bitch. She just had to wait. I'm looking after you. Aren't I?' He looks at her.

She nods again.

'I'm feeding you. You got a roof over your head.'

He squints at the picture. 'I broke my glasses. That's why I can't read it. I can't see a thing.' He throws the paper down.

'Useless bitch, you are. Can't even read. I don't know why your mum got those sluts working for her now. She sends these fat cows, Eloise's a fat-arsed cow. Your mum should come herself. Like she used to. We got on good. Me and Amber. Amber and me.'

He lifts his Coke can to his mouth. The big lump in his throat moves up and down as he swallows. 'Ahh, good,' he says. Then he bolts up straight. 'What day is it?'

The day after Rachel's party, Bree-Anna thinks to herself. Three days until Christmas.

'What day is it?' He grabs her arm, lifts her off the floor, and squeezes it tight. Bree-Anna squeals. She shakes her head.

He drops her and walks to the door and back again. 'It was Sunday you came to visit. The shops were closed. So, it was Sunday. That was yesterday?' He waits for her to answer. 'That was yesterday?' he yells.

She nods.

He paces back to the door and turns to face her. 'Today is Monday. Fuck it. Tomorrow is Tuesday.'

He bites his bottom lip.

'We got to call your mother,' he says, his eyes big and wide.

Bree-Anna leaps forward. 'Now?'

He disappears through the door, leaving it wide open. Bree-Anna rushes at it in case he comes back to close and lock it again. He is calling her mother. This is her chance.

He holds a finger up and she stops in the doorway. 'You stay right there, young lady.'

The olden-day phone is connected to the wall and will never reach all the way to her. He picks up the receiver, his finger hovering over the buttons.

Bree-Anna jiggles in the doorway, excitement bubbling through her like soft drink.

'What's the number?' he asks.

Her excitement thuds flat, squashed by a brick. They told her in school they should remember their phone numbers and addresses, just in case they ever got lost, but she never learnt it.

He shakes his head at her, his bushy eyebrows pulling together. 'You really are the dumbest, most useless...' He sighs. Puts down the receiver. Scratches his head. 'Maybe... stay fuckin' there.' He points at her and goes to the kitchen.

She hears him rattling open drawers, throwing stuff on the floor, swearing, then he shouts, 'You little beauty.'

Back in the loungeroom, he beckons her over and hands her a business card. 'I broke my glasses,' he says.

Bree-Anna touches the smooth purple card, the gleaming gold writing. Her mother's name. Her mother's phone number.

'You dial it,' he says, lifting the receiver to his ear.

Bree-Anna knows enough to read the numbers. She presses the buttons to what she knows go to her mother's mobile phone. She hears the ringing sound muffled from where he holds the phone against his ear.

Click. A voice. She jumps up and down and holds out her hand.

He bangs the phone back in the cradle. 'Fuckin' message bank. I hate those things.' He kicks the phone table and it tumbles over. The phone lies on the floor. Bree-Anna can hear it—*beep beep beep*. Not broken. Her body tingles. She turns her mother's card around and around in her hand.

He flops on the lounge and thumps the arm rest with his fist. 'Fucking answering machines. Rude bitch. Why doesn't she pick up? Fuck her.' He throws a DVD case on the floor. The disk flies out and skims over the carpet.

'Tomorrow really is Tuesday?' he asks. 'You're sure?'

Bree-Anna has no idea. 'Yes,' she says. 'Tuesday.'

He rubs his hands over his face and stands up. He grunts as he bends to pick up the table and the phone, puts it all back together and stands over it, his hands on either side of the table as if he expects it to all leap off the floor without his kicking. 'Okay,' he says. 'Dial it again.'

Bree-Anna reads the numbers, presses them into the phone. He holds the receiver to his ear. She can talk to a message bank. He should let her do it.

Ring Ring.

Ring Ring.

Ring Ring.

Click.

The quiet sound of her mother.

He doesn't talk.

Bree-Anna gulps a breath, tears burning at her eyes.

'Um,' he says.

'Um,' he says again.

'T-t-tuesday,' he stutters.

He pulls the phone away from his ear. Bangs it on his thigh. Mumbles and swears, 'Shit, fuck,' blows out a breath.

Puts the phone back to his mouth.

'T-t-ell Eloise n-n-not to c-c-come.'

And he hangs up the phone.

Bree-Anna stares up at him, tears draining from her eyes. He kicks the table and it rocks, but stays upright.

'I hate shittin' answering machines,' he says.

Eloise parks at the front of Amber's house, which looks like the same dumpy brick box as always, not like a place where a disaster is in the process of playing out, except for the cop car parked out the front. What had she expected? A throng of media? Had they been and gone? CWA ladies with casseroles? The cops searching the yard?

Eloise's stomach churns with nervousness, probably still churning from the phone call from her useless junkie brother, if truth be known. He's best out of their lives, and she shoves him from her thoughts. What will Amber be like? A blubbering mess? Her usual flippant self? That seems unlikely. Eloise wills herself to open the car door. She's got to do it.

Her phone chirps a message: *You got a shift at lunch time? I'm coming by work, hope to see you then xxoo*

She grins. A visit from Mike makes the day worthwhile. She gets out the car and walks along the chipped concrete path and texts back: *Hey sexy got a double shift cu in the office xxxxxooooo and more.*

A cop answers Amber's door. A chick cop, narrow-shouldered like she couldn't catch a criminal if her life depended on it. She glances at Eloise and then looks past her, up and down the street, and finally she looks Eloise in the eye.

'Who are you?'

'Eloise. I'm a friend of Amber's. I just came to see if she needed anything.'

'Wait.' The cop closes the door. Eloise taps her phone against the thigh and waits, the sun searing on the back of her neck. Finally, the cop opens the door again and steps aside, pointing and saying, 'In the kitchen.'

Eloise steps inside and is assailed by the smell of stale ashtrays and shut-in heat. The Christmas tree glints in the darkness surrounded by a sprawl of presents. What will happen to Bree-Anna's presents? How depressing! Maybe they will find her alive.

Amber doesn't even bother to look up when Eloise enters the kitchen. Skinny Amber always looks like she needs a good feed; today she looks downright haggard. Half-dead, like the worms have already had a feed. Eloise has no idea what all those men see in her. Except, of course, her legs open so readily.

'Amber?'

Amber lifts her head and clutches her empty coffee cup tighter. 'What? You hear something?'

'Um...' Eloise pulls out a chair and sits. 'No, I just came by. See if you needed anything.'

Amber nods her head and lifts the cup to her mouth, realises it's empty, lowers her hand. The cup wobbles on the table.

Eloise reaches over to catch it. 'How about I make you another coffee?' she says. 'Something to eat? You eaten?'

Amber bites down on her lip, her eyes vacant, lights a cigarette.

'Righto then.' Eloise rises and locates the jug. She moves filthy dishes aside to fit the jug under the tap. No one in their right mind would hire one of Amber's 'Chicks Who Clean' if they saw the pigsty Amber herself lived in. Eloise likes to think when she no longer needs to be one of those chicks who clean, she'll tell everyone how grotty Amber is. She turns. Amber's shoulders hunch over the table, her pointy shoulder blades poking out of her T-shirt. Maybe not.

'Milk? Sugar?' Eloise bangs through the cupboards until she finds a clean coffee cup. The tea and coffee makings are spread over the kitchen bench, easy to find. 'Is there any bread? I can make you a sandwich. And Declan too. Is Declan here?' She opens the bread bin, the fridge, the pantry. There are mostly packets of chips and biscuits and a few cans of baked beans. Milk in the fridge, some yoghurt, out of date. 'You want me to do some shopping for you?'

Amber stares ahead, sucking on a cigarette, her mouth wrinkled like an old woman. Eloise sighs and makes the coffee sweet and milky regardless of Amber's preferences. Robot-like,

Amber clasps the coffee in one hand and cigarette in the other, alternating suck and sip.

'Is there anything else you need? Some banking, contacting clients?' Anything better than bloody cleaning. 'I gotta go to town tomorrow, pick up some prints. I can drop into the bank. If you need me to.'

The mobile phone on the table sings, *girls just wanna have fu-un, oh girls just wanna have fun...* Amber glances sideways at it, blinks and slurps her coffee, breathes in her cigarette.

'Aren't you going to answer it?'

'It's just that goddam abortion, Randall,' Amber croaks.

Declan slinks into the room and lolls on the door frame. Eloise smiles at him and he tries to smile back, his dark face and glistening lips still handsome despite everything. The older he gets, the more he looks like his dad. Such a pity what happened to his dad. Hard to say if Bree-Anna looked like her dad, seeing as no one knows who he is. Well, maybe Amber knows.

Amber's phone rings again. Amber slides it toward her, stares at the screen until it stops ringing.

'What if...?' Eloise says. W*hat if it's someone with news?* she wants to say.

'It's Randall again.'

'Okay.' Eloise scratches her elbow, looks at her watch, and wonders if she has time to do the washing up.

The phone beeps to show Randall left a message.

Amber spins the mobile in circles, watching the screen as if searching for a better call, one with news worth hearing, a call from the police to say they found her, alive and well, a call from a friend to say she was there all along. Would the police ring Amber or would they just radio the cop in the lounge and tell her? What was that cop doing there, anyway? Fat help she was.

Shouldn't she be out there interviewing witnesses or something?

'I thought the media would be here—to help, you know, get the word out there.'

'They were. I spoke to them this morning. A press conference.' Amber twists the last words in a snarl. 'If you bothered to turn on your TV, Eloise, you would have seen me.'

'Right,' says Eloise.

'And I don't want them hanging around here like a bad smell. That's what the cop is for. To keep them away.'

'I wondered what she was for.'

Amber picks up the phone and flips it around and around in her hand, devours a lungful of stinking smoke and blows it over Eloise.

Eloise covers her mouth and coughs, resisting the urge to frown. 'You want me to do that washing up for you?'

'No, no,' Amber says. 'Declan will do it. Declan,' she calls out loud as though she hasn't seen him loitering in the doorway. Eloise looks around at him, but he doesn't move or blink, or say a word.

Eloise reaches out to still Amber's hand. The hand freezes stiff. 'They'll find her. Don't worry. There's so many people looking, they'll find her.'

Amber plucks her hand from Eloise's light grip and scrolls through her phone. Deep lines crease between her brow and Eloise regrets her words, a catalyst for ensuing tears. She doesn't want to deal with tears. She takes a deep breath, searching for a topic, not off-topic from the elephant in the room, but distracting, helpful, anything.

'I thought your mum might be here,' she says. 'Has your mum been here?'

Amber grunts and concentrates on composing a text.

'Who are you texting?' Declan pipes up from his door jamb.

'Glen,' Amber says sharply.

'Glen?' Eloise says. 'Glen Fitz? Are you seeing him now?'

Amber doesn't reply.

Eloise glances around at Declan, who slinks away. Glen Fitz, pretty boy dreadlocks and too many piercings, rocked into town six months ago and stirred up all the single young things at the pub. Something about him gave Eloise the creeps though. He got her spider senses crawling when he came into the pub.

'What about your mum? You talked to your mum. I mean, I know you and her... but under the circumstances...'

Amber drops the phone with a *clunk*. 'What! Give her the satisfaction.'

'Satisfaction?'

'She'd gloat!'

'Oh no.' Eloise reaches toward Amber's hands and they disappear under the table. 'I'm sure she wouldn't. She loved Bree.' The past tense is out and she can't think how to fix it. 'Your mum would want to be here. I'm sure you just have to ask.'

Better than relying on Glen Fitz, stoner pretty boy. Seriously, how does this woman manage to run a successful cleaning business and make such stupid decisions about men? It's like she's smart and dumb in one scrawny head.

Amber brings her hand out from under the table, shakes cigarette ash onto a plate with congealed sauce and chicken nuggets, and nods toward the landline phone. 'Besides,' she says, 'That's the number she knows, that's the number they made her memorise.'

'Your mum?'

'Nooo.' Amber twists her hands into her hair and tugs violently at it. 'Sometimes, Eloise, I don't know how you were ever smart enough to get into uni.'

The bully Amber never far away, thinks Eloise, even at a time like this. 'Not your mum?' She rests back in the chair and sighs, playing her part.

'No, Eloise, you idiot.' Amber bites smoke out of the cigarette and smashes it dead into the plate. 'Bree-Anna!' She huffs the smoke out of her lungs with the girl's name. 'Bree-Anna will ring on that phone. The landline.' She points, her nails long with chipped black polish. 'That is the number they made her memorise in prep. Her teacher told me. She came this morning and said they made all the kids remember their phone number and address.'

Eloise nods and pushes back her chair. 'I got to...'

A pile of paper plops onto the table beside her, and Bree-Anna, hair poking unbrushed out from her head, fat cheeked and freckled, looks up from the posters.

Declan hovers near them, nudges them closer to Eloise.

Eloise rests her hand on his forearm. 'These are great, Declan. Did you do these?'

'The cops got 'em,' he says in a low voice, and biting his nail he adds, 'I found the photo but. It's her school photo.'

'You want me to take them?'

He nods and she stands, pulling the posters to her chest.

'I got a shift at the pub in ten minutes. I'll be late.' She focuses on Amber, but Amber's still got the landline phone in her sights, willing it to ring. 'You call me. Anytime. If you need anything. Okay?' She turns and rubs Declan's forearm and his father's brown eyes look up her. Damn him, he is the spitting image. 'I'll come by tomorrow. There'll be good news by then.'

'Don't you go calling my mother,' Amber calls after her as she leaves the room.

The cop opens the door for her. She tells Eloise if she's heading east there is still a road block where they are searching beside the highway. It might be there all day, or more. Eloise steps in the blinding sun, a boulder in her stomach. What will they find on the highway in the long grass? What are the chances of finding the kid? Next to none. She is shit at this supportive-friend-slash-employee thing. But who else does Amber have? Glen Fitz is probably too stoned to even know what's going on. Amber needs her mother. She might be an old hippie who lives in a stinking house with dog shit and cat fur but she loves those kids. And probably Amber too. Did when she was a kid, supported her even though she was pregnant and in high school. Whatever they fell out over surely can be put aside now. As soon as she gets a break at work, she'll call Amber's mother, no matter what Amber says, and tell her get her arse over here.

MONDAY NIGHT

Bree-Anna still has her mother's business card. She keeps it flat against her sweaty palm, but with her fingers closed over it so he can't see it. He sits in the bedroom with her, on the floor, his back pressed on the door. He's collected up all the jewellery and has it spread out on the carpet between his legs.

'See these.' He holds up a pair of square golden things in a box. They're too big and ugly to wear as earrings. 'These are mine. The old fart who does my trust account sent me them for Christmas one year. He sends something every year. You know what they are?'

Bree-Anna presses her teeth on the thumb and sucks harder. She rests her head on the wall and is reminded of the tender lump on the back of her head. She lifts her head away. Afternoon sunlight streams through the window above her and makes a rectangle across the oven-like room. Dust floats in the sunlight.

'They're cuff links.' He laughs and twirls them around in their case. 'You tell me, what am I supposed to do with cuff links? Silly old goat.' He turns his head from side to side and the bones in his neck crack. 'They're gold but, so I keep 'em.

Aiilleen'—he stretches the name out—'says they're not real gold. But they're gold. Aileen is just jealous. She wanted our mother's rings, but I hide them when she comes.' He throws the cuff links into the jewellery box. 'It's funny when she comes, watching her lookin' but trying to look like she's not lookin'. Greedy bitch. She used to come every month lookin' for those rings. She don't come so much anymore. Not since she organised cleaning for me. That was when your mum first started coming. I got Aileen to thank for that.'

He packs the jewellery, one piece at a time, back into the glossy case. He takes the brooch out of his pocket and throws it in too. He grunts as he stands and reaches up to the suitcase on top of the wardrobe. Bree-Anna breathes deeply through her nose and out again.

'Don't get too excited,' he says as he grins and puts the suitcase down on the bed. He opens the suitcase and tilts his head to the side with a crunching sound. 'Now where did this come from?' He holds up Baby, his fingers around her neck, her legs dangling.

Bree-Anna breathes fast, sucks hard on her thumb and digs her fingernails into the carpet. With a laugh like the baddie in a cartoon he pretends to walk Baby toward her, then cutting himself off mid-laugh, he throws Baby back in the suitcase, carefully puts the jewellery case beside her, and clicks the latches.

Bree-Anna knows he isn't really going to give Baby back. Mr Randall enjoys teasing her. She knows about teasing because of Declan. And the boys at school. 'Don't take the bait,' Mummy said to her one day when she cried and cried because Declan tricked her into thinking it was a school day when really it was Saturday. Bree-Anna, dressed in her school uniform, packed biscuits into her lunch box because Mummy wasn't up yet and

Declan stood in his pyjamas laughing at her, calling her a 'dumb dodo bird'.

She didn't understand. 'Like a stupid fish, taking the bait,' her mother said. 'If he knows he is getting to you, he will keep doing it.'

So, when the boys at school call her 'fatty fatty bum bum', or Declan plays a trick on her, she laughs or pretends she doesn't care.

Mr Randall is a man. A skinny man with hairy eyebrows and pants that are too big and she can see inside his pants and she knows he is hairy like a man not a boy. But in his head, he is like a boy. A boy who thinks it is funny to tease little girls. To pretend they are going to talk to their mummy, but then to just talk about not having the cleaner come. I am not a stupid fish, Bree-Anna decides. Though he made her want to jump up and grab Baby, hug her and hug her, she pretends she doesn't care. *Sorry Baby.*

He puts the suitcase back on the wardrobe, high up out of her reach and flops, lying spread out all over the bed. Bree-Anna tries hard not to look at the door.

She has to make him forget to lock the door. She pulls on her thumb, swallowing with little clicks in the back of her mouth. *Go to sleep. Go to sleep.* She closes her eyes and pretends she has a dandelion fairy and wishes. *Mr Randall, go to sleep, go to sleep.* She turns the card in her hand, around and around in her hand, wishing.

She wishes for a long time, and then quiet as the quietest mouse in the world, she lifts herself off the floor and peers up onto the bed.

His eyes stare straight back at her. He grins.

She smiles back at him and drops back down to the floor.

'Come and keep me company.'

She can hear him patting the mattress. She squeezes her

eyes tight closed, squashes the card in her fist. *Go to sleep, go to sleep.*

'Girlie,' he says and, startled, she opens her eyes. He hangs over the edge of the bed and waggles his finger at her. 'Come on.'

Bree-Anna bites her lip and turns onto her hands and knees. She crawls toward the bed, and at the exact time she is by the bed, she drops back to sit on her legs. She smiles at him, and while she is smiling, she tucks Mummy's card under the bed. She keeps smiling. He doesn't notice what she did. He spins on the bed and sits with his legs planted on the floor. He pushes his hands under her arms, presses into her sides, and lifts her onto the bed.

'You're one heavy lump,' he says, pretending to breathe heavy like he ran a long race.

Bree-Anna pulls the nightie over her knees, hugs her legs to her chest. The newspaper with her face on the front messes in with the unmade bed.

He sits on the edge of the bed, tilts his head to the side, and his eyes move up and down and over her. She wraps her arms tighter around her knees.

'You like that nightie?' he asks.

She nods her head.

'It's not very sexy,' he says, resting his chin in his hand.

Bree-Anna shakes her head, pressing her heels to her body.

'And the necklace I gave you. You're still wearing that?'

She stretches the neck of her nightie so he can see the necklace.

'Mmm.' He nods. 'You know, I don't think you said thank you for them gifts.'

Bree-Anna clenches her fists to stop her thumb from going in her mouth.

'Say thank you,' he says, only half his mouth smiling.

'Thank you,' she says.

He thrusts his face at her. 'Thank you *what?*'

'Thank you, Mr Randall,' Bree-Anna breathes quietly.

He sits back and leans on the headboard. 'I like it when you call me Mr Randall. Everyone else calls me Colin. I hate that name. Weak. I should have been called Mick, or Jack, or Jake. A strong name. The kids at school...' He grabs a pillow and hugs it to his stomach. 'You get teased at school? I bet you do, looking how you do. The pudgy ones always get teased.' He bends toward her and pokes her leg. 'They still got them same toilets at that school? I went to school in Stinky Gully. Did I tell you that?'

Bree-Anna shakes her head and her thumb creeps into her mouth.

'Them toilets.' He grins, his lips pulled together, no teeth showing. 'I was in the girl's toilet once.' He throws the pillow aside and shakes his finger at her. 'Never you mind why I was there, I was just there, all right? Well, this girl came to our school in grade three. I remember it was grade three because I had that dragon Mrs Chance in grade three. This girl came from New South Wales. They're all sluts down there. This girl came out of the toilet cubicle and she just looks at me and I think, oh damn I'm busted. I'm gonna get a canin' from my dad. That Mrs Chance was always running to my mum and tellin' her stuff about me and that bitch always got to tell my dad. But this girl just says "show me yours and I'll show you mine"—just like that. I didn't know what to do, but then I just pull down my shorts and show her my undies. "That's just your undies," she says, just like a slut. So, I pull down my undies and...' He waves his hand in front of his pants.

'Well, she went red as a beetroot. I said, now you gotta show me yours and she lifts up her uniform, just like that, and I say that's just your knickers, and so she pulls the front of her knickers down and I saw her fanny all smooth with a dark crack in it where the piss comes out. That how you look? You got hair down there? No, you too little. Baby, baby sucky thumb.'

Bree-Anna pulls out her thumb and swallows, her legs pulled so close her chin rests on her knees.

'She left our school not long after that. Pauline, her name was.' He leans back and the bed head tilts toward the wall. He fingers the newspaper, his dancing walking fingers bringing it closer. His tongue rolls around in his mouth. 'So, gives us a look then.'

The newspaper? She scrambles to shuffle the pages near her toward him.

He lifts his legs onto the bed and wraps them around her, his heels in her back. 'Come 'ere.' He bends his knees, trying to slide her toward him, but the sheets and bedspread just rumple beneath. He sighs and grabs her ankles and hauls her closer, the bed clothes coming along too. Her body falls backward and she flings her hands out behind to catch herself.

Knees in the air, her back arched, he yanks her ankles, and she collapses back against his feet.

'Sit up.' He squeezes his nails into her calves, his voice harsh.

She struggles up to sit, now pinned between his triangled knees. He tugs at the hem of her nightie. She snatches it back down. She had no undies. Her wet pants went out the door with her pink shorts. She wants undies. She kicks with her feet, her heels digging into the bed, trying to push herself back down the bed, but he holds her in with his heels. He grabs each of her shoulders and jabs his thumbs into her.

She twists and squeals, 'You're hurting me.' His other four fingers gouge into her shoulder blades; with a cry of pain her heel springs out from her and she kicks him.

He releases her, his hands clutching where her foot got him. Tears squeeze from the edges of his pinched together eyes. 'You bitch,' he gasps and falls onto the bed, holding his hands over his wee-wee. Right where it hurts. That is what Declan would say.

He rolls his body into a ball. Bree-Anna scrambles away to the end of the bed, and panting, she lets herself drop off the side onto the floor. Scuttling on her hands and knees, she crosses the room and squashes herself in the corner between the wall and the dresser.

She sobs. The sunlight isn't coming in the window anymore, but somewhere out there, dandelion fairies dance, people get in and out of cars and do their shopping. She swallows her sobs. Be quiet. Let him go to sleep. She scans under the bed. The bedspread drapes over the floor at the end of the bed, but toward the top, the shadow of her mother's card, bent and folded, waits for her.

The same unemployed no-hopers, pokie addicts, and dullards fritter away their lives and lunch time in the pub. They all want to talk about Amber and the fat kid. *What's her name again?* they ask. 'Bree-Anna,' Eloise says for the hundredth time. She wants to tell them if they are so interested, why aren't they out there with the SES scouring the grass for clues, or... Damn it, she left the posters in the car. Well, not much use putting them in here; everyone already knows what is going on. She'll take them to town tomorrow—if they haven't found Bree-Anna yet. Everyone wants to know what the heck the little kid was doing walking along the highway on her own, and Eloise shrugs because if you can't say something nice, say nothing at all.

The door slides open with a *shh* sound and fans a blast of

humid December air. Eloise holds her breath, but some guys in fluoro vests amble in, not Mike. She could ask Mike what she should do about Anthony. Mike will say forget him, junkie waste of space. If she thinks it often enough, she will forget he is her brother with a flair for music and an ear for the new and fantastic. Well, that he was, and is no more. The sadness of him losing his passion, that he was the one who could tell her what to listen to and be stunned with magic melodies, that he could take her places, dark and full of dance, are a time gone by. He will never be that brother again.

The burliest orange vested man rests his tattooed forearms on the bar. 'What'll you have?' she asks.

'Four pots,' he says, 'and you got a lunch special?'

She points to the end of the bar. 'Go and see Maggie on that one, she'll sort you out.'

'Sure,' he says, leaning on the bar and raising his eyebrows, 'but what's good?'

'Oh, everything's good,' she says, because flirting back brings in the customers. Apparently. So Mike says.

The guy grunts, already disinterested. He takes the beers off to their table and she figures they won't be going back to work this afternoon. Christmas, the heat, summer, sends everyone a bit loopy and lazy.

One of them seems familiar. He nods at her as though he knows her and she nods back, trying to place him. A younger him, shorter hair… Oh yeah, Mitchell Jackson. They were in the same year at school. She smiles at him, and he smiles and looks down at his beer, wipes the condensation from the glass, a shy boy still. She laughs to herself, remembering how Amber gave him a hard time. He sat in front of them in Business Studies. Amber's main aim of the lesson was to get Mitchell's face to burn red with embarrassment. It didn't take much. 'Oh, Mitchell, you've got a new haircut. Sexy,' or 'Mitchell, I forgot my pen, can I borrow one of yours? I promise I won't suck on it.' Poor guy. It's a wonder Amber ever passed Business Studies—she paid so little attention, but she topped the class most times. It was the only subject she beat Eloise in. Eloise, head down, after the score that would get her into Law, and Amber out drinking and fucking and getting pregnant. Nothing has changed. Still the centre of attention. In the news. Her daughter on posters, being shared all over Facebook, on the news. Still, not really what she would have wished on Amber. Or anyone.

The door bursts open and this time Eloise's insides spark with anticipation. Mike at last. Followed by, the flame doused in an instant, his goddamned wife. He didn't mention that in his text. Trailing behind, worse oh worse, his two kids.

The kids, perfectly blonde girls, perfectly dressed, perfectly behaved (of course), take a quiet seat in the corner, and Mike, dashing, handsome, hair just a bit longer than usual, probably the only man in town that day actually wearing a suit, and certainly the only one in this stinking town able to pull it off, strolls toward the bar, the gleam in his eye unseen by his double D wife in her designer clothes and too much make-up.

'Sonja,' he says, 'you remember Eloise.'

'Oh, we've met before?' Sonja holds out a limp hand with dangling cold fingertips and says, 'I'm not sure. Have we met before, Mike?'

Mike laughs a little nervously, doing that thing where he smooths the skin on his chin as though he has a beard to comb. 'Yes, you remember, Eloise is trying to get into photography school.'

'A Bachelor of Fine Arts,' Eloise says through a gritted smile. Why is he doing this to her? To them?

'Oh, I meet so many people, it is hard to remember.' Sonja shakes her head, eyes to the ceiling. 'You must forgive me.

Mike, dear,' she rests her hand on his sleeve, 'have you stocked any decent Sauvignons in this place yet?'

'Not much call for it in here,' Eloise says. 'I'll go and see what's in the bottle shop.'

'Oh no, no, Mike, you go and choose, you know what I like,' Sonja says, stroking Mike's shoulder.

'Sure.' Mike covers her hand in his and looks at Eloise, grinning, the one crooked tooth she finds so enticing, the imperfection that makes him perfect. Damn him to hell. 'A couple of lemonades for the girls and you know what I like.'

'Um, Scotch?'

'Bourbon and Coke,' he says flatly, because she knows this, but why would he flaunt that fact in front of Sonja? Does he enjoy living dangerously? Ha! She knows the answer to that.

'Bourbon and Coke, the best we've got, boss,' she says with a salute.

Both women, the legitimate and the other woman, watch his broad shoulders sway toward the bottle shop. Eloise sloshes lemonade into a glass, her usual deftness turned to butter fingers. Sonja fingers the glittering jewel (a diamond?) on the end of her necklace. Eloise flicks another glass upright and fizzes a second lemonade.

'I remember, you're the one who's a cleaner,' Sonja says.

'I help out an old school friend with her cleaning business.' Eloise pours a generous double bourbon.

'Oh, the one with the lost little girl.' Sonja turns her head and glances at her own perfectly perfect offspring. 'Just terrible. And so close to Christmas. When family is so important.'

She knows, thinks Eloise. Why would she say that if she didn't know?

'Amber's taking it hard.' Eloise splashes a dash of Coke into the bourbon—not a full glass, just the way he likes it—and puts it on the bar. They both stare at the glass and the message of intimacy it sends.

'Thanks... um, Angela?'

'Eloise.'

'Of course, Eloise. Can I have a tray for these?'

Eloise puts the drinks on a tray, and without another word, Sonja joins her politely smiling, A-plus, ballet-dancing, saying-thank-you-Mummy children.

Mike comes back and behind the bar, with what could only be called a mediocre Sauvignon. 'This is crap,' he says. 'Who does the orders for this place?'

'You do,' Eloise says, flinging the bar cloth down. 'What on earth are you doing bringing her here?'

'She insisted,' Mike says, unscrewing the lid from the wine bottle. 'She's my wife—she can come to the pub,' he tosses the screw cap in the bin, 'which she owns a part of.'

Eloise reaches up and hands him a wine glass. He holds it up to the light and hands it back. She hands him another. 'This one clean enough for *her*?'

'Probably not,' he grins and licks his lips, presses them together, the shine wet and red, 'but we'll give it a go.' He pours the pee-coloured wine into the glass, *glug glugging* between them. The glass full, he turns away from her and calls over his shoulder, 'Send Maggie over to take our lunch order, will you?'

'Yes, sir!' She salutes him again.

He turns back, the glass held between elegant fingers. 'Don't worry, after lunch I'll need you to take me through the receipts from last week. There are some anomalies.'

'What's she going to think about that?'

'In the office. After we've eaten lunch,' he replies.

Eloise pours beers, gives change for the pokies, wipes the bar, one eye to the corner table, Sonja pulling something wrong in the lunch from her mouth and placing it on the side of her plate with a disgusted look toward the kitchen. Him touching his daughter's hair, ironing it golden and shining while the girl jigs in her chair, staring up and chattering at him, doting, in love with her good-looking generous father.

Done eating, he leaves the table, a peck on Sonja's over-made foundation-coloured cheek, and not an acknowledgement toward Eloise. Eloise waits. She bears the burden of not looking at the corridor heading toward the office. Busy, busy with wiping the bar. Sonja watches him, glances at her. Busy, busy she offers drinks to all those with nearly empty glasses. At last, the interval no longer appearing urgent, she calls to Maggie that Mike needs her to go through some receipts from last week, can she watch the bar? Maggie smiles sweetly because that is the way Maggie is. Too sweet for her own good. A good cover.

She opens the door to the office-slash-storeroom. He lolls, his feet on the dusty desk, rarely used for office work because he does most of it in his other pub, closer to his home. The city pub that no doubt has the right sort of Sauvignons for Sonja.

'How's Amber?' he asks straight up.

Bloody Amber, everyone wants to know how Amber is.

'She's not good.' Eloise sits on the edge of the desk.

'Smart cookie.' He folds his legs off the desk onto the floor and pats his lap. 'She could have gone far if she hadn't taken up dropping sprogs left, right, and centre. I hope they find the kid.'

'It's not looking good,' Eloise says, moving to his lap.

'No, it's not.' He pinches her nipple between his fingertips and she is a puddle of glossy melted chocolate.

Eloise explores the prickle of hair on his cheek. 'I think she knows.'

'So what if she does?'

His mouth warm, his tongue insistent, his hand squeezing

her breast, sends a careless sizzle through her. She pulls away. 'I don't think I locked the door.'

He catches her mouth with his, nibbles and bites on her lip. She grabs his crotch firm, elated with the feel of him growing beneath her hand, his need for her so great.

He undoes the top button of her jeans and slips his hand inside. Her spine lifts from her hips and arches, a jet of breath gushing into her.

The door crashes open and Eloise jumps up, pulling her T-shirt over her open jeans. Mike wheels his chair up to the desk and scrambles for a random piece of paper.

Maggie looks from her to him and hisses, 'She's coming.'

Sonja appears at the door, not a hair askew. 'Mike darling, there's *no one* behind the bar.'

'I'm going,' Maggie says and scuttles away.

Mike straightens a pile of paper with a bang of the dust on the desk. 'Nearly done here.'

Eloise crosses her hands across her open jeans, her heart thumping like loose iron in a storm.

'And the girls are getting restless. You promised them we'd be back in time for a swim before we go and see the Christmas lights.'

'I said,' Mike's elbows thud onto the desk, 'we are nearly done.'

Sonja's head nods up and down like a bobble-headed doll, and Eloise almost has a pang of guilt when a gleam of wet shimmers in the rim of her eyes. Then Sonja says, 'The bar is filthy,' and the guilt kicks away with the clatter of Sonja's heels down the corridor.

Mike sighs and gets up. 'You working tomorrow?'

Eloise does up her pants, her pulsing libido left hanging. 'Just cleaning jobs, and I got to go to town and pick up some prints. We could meet in town.'

'Maybe.' Mike checks his pockets, keys, wallet, unable to look at her. The mix of sadness, regret, and when he finally looks up at her, dissipated lust mixed like paint on his face. She wishes she had her camera.

'I've still got to get a portrait, a character study for my portfolio. Remember you said you might...'

'After Christmas,' he says. 'It's manic at the moment.'

'I'm already late.' She rubs her arms suddenly, explicably cold. 'They gave me an extension—because of what happened with Dad.'

'How is your dad?' he asks, checking again for the keys in his pocket that haven't gone anywhere.

'Same.'

'Right, that's good then,' he says and pecks her cheek, even though it is not good. Not good at all.

'Tomorrow?'

'I'll let you know,' he says and leaves her in the dust and empty boxes of the windowless room.

'Yep,' she says, though he's long gone down the corridor.

Mr Randall moans and complains. It sounds like pretend, like when Declan doesn't want to go to school. Bree-Anna presses herself hard against the wall. The wall presses hard back. She sticks her fingers in her ears and only hears the roaring of air in her head. She rocks back and forth and wishes, wishes, wishes... wishes she was in her bedroom. She closes her eyes, makes the picture in her head, the curtains with stripes, three different colours of pink, from light to dark, orange, gold, and one purple with gold dots. In the morning, sun shines through the curtains and makes a pattern on her bed. On her bed, her orange octopus that used to be Mummy's when she was little, a white fluffy dog her grandma gave her that has a zipper for putting pyjamas in, but Bree-Anna never does, she always forgets, and Baby (*oh poor Baby*), from the bed Mr Randall spits *bitch—you don't care*, and Bree-Anna's teeth crunch together... what else... a teddy bear she doesn't know where it came from, his feet bang down on the floor. Bree-Anna remembers a dog with floppy ears she calls Midgy for no reason, a woolly sheep she calls Sheepy. Some of them might be on the floor, from when she kicks them when she sleeps.

His feet bang closer, stomping loud on purpose.

The little table next to her bed is white with round pink handles. In the top drawer, she keeps undies and socks; in the next middle drawer, pyjamas and nighties; in the bottom drawer...

He stands over where she is squeezed between the wall and the dressing table, and leans on the wobbling dresser.

In the bottom drawer... why can't she remember?

He swings back his foot, and she turns and hides her face, and his toes smash into her thigh.

'There, bitch,' he says, 'we're even now.'

He kicks her three more times, on the same part of her leg, and her head knocks on the wall.

Now I owe you, she thinks, but doesn't say it. Her tears are hot on her face, but she makes sure they are quiet tears because she is not a stupid fish. *I owe you forever,* she thinks and curls tighter into the corner.

In her bottom drawer she keeps Baby's clothes. How could she forget?

Her carpet is cream, or white maybe; she has a rug with daises, but she doesn't know how many daisies. She has eight books. She counted them. Three books her grandma gave her, four books that Declan didn't want anymore, and one book she made Mummy buy from the newsagent. Her toy box is white too, with pictures of princesses on the outside. It is always too hard to find things in the toy box so she likes to keep favourite things outside of the box. Mainly in the box are things she doesn't feel like playing with much.

He leaves the room; she doesn't hear the door close. Could it be open?

A book she likes is *The Ugly Duckling*. They teased and didn't like the Duckling, but it got them back when it became a beautiful swan. She's got *Beauty and the Beast* too, but not the story book, a search-and-find book, with busy pictures and you have to find the things in pictures, like Belle and the teapots—Mrs Potts and the Beast. Bree-Anna knows where they all are.

He comes back in, dragging something heavy and grunting. She hears him fiddling about on the wall on the other side of the dresser. Then *pop,* she hears the television come to life. He puts in a DVD and goes back to the bed. She recognises the same movie from yesterday. Muddy orcs and the bony thing that reminds her of Mr Randall.

The light fades and the sunset glows red through the window. Bree-Anna remembers in her head everything in her bedroom, then her mother's room, then the kitchen and the loungeroom, even the bathroom. Especially she remembers Mummy's room and the colours of the make-up and the necklaces and earrings and the shoes in pairs, or muddled at the bottom of the wardrobe.

Around her the room grows grey. Noises like mice rattle in the walls. She closes her eyes.

Bree-Anna wakes, stiff and cramped. The light from the TV flickers over the dark room. The DVD has finished and the beginning part, where you are meant to press play is going over and over. She straightens her legs and winces at the pain in her kicked thigh. She crawls forward, out of her corner.

In the flashing light she can see his lump in the bed. Sleeping? She crawls, creeping over the floor to the bed. He snorts, and she stops still. No sound comes from the bed, as though he is holding his breath. Bree-Anna holds her breath. Then his breath comes out in a loud snore.

She crawls again, her thigh stiff with pain every time that knee takes her weight. She feels about on the dusty carpet under the bed and finds nothing—where is it? Did he find it while she was sleeping? Then like a miracle, her hand touches the card. With fumbling fingers, she hugs it to her chest.

The door.

Behind the TV, the door is closed.

But is it locked?

She crawls along the side of the bed, listening for his snores and grunts. His noises sound like sobs, as though he is crying. She freezes and presses against the bed as though it will hide her. She knows it won't. It is like how ostriches put their heads in the sand and think that is enough. Her heart thumps and she wonders if ostriches also think their beating hearts will give them away. He is crying. Crying and sleeping at the same time. It gives her a funny feeling in her tummy to hear him. Like she is hearing a secret.

At the end of the bed, she stands slowly and limps and feels her way around the table he dragged in with the TV, still playing the same music over and over.

Her palms touch the door, flat on the wood. She gropes across to the handle, cool and metal in her hand, and she turns it. The handle turns, the door gives and opens. A giggle escapes her, and she clamps her hand over her mouth. She looks up toward the wardrobe. *Not long, Baby.*

Bree-Anna opens the door; slow and steady wins the race, she thinks. She is the tortoise not the hare. She squeezes between the gap and into the loungeroom. Moonlight pours through the window, the furniture creepy and ghostlike, and a space where the TV used to be. On tiptoes she sneaks to the phone on the little table by the kitchen door. She lifts the receiver and it chirps loud and she thinks it might wake him. She covers the little holes with her hand and drops to her knees.

How late is it? Will her mum be sleeping too? Has she got her mobile phone beside her bed? Is there a man sleeping there too? She holds the card toward the moonlight coming in the window and pushes the buttons on the phone.

Ring Ring.

Ring Ring.

So loud.

Bree-Anna stares at the door to the bedroom.

Ring Ring.

Click.

This is Amber from 'Chicks Who Clean'. Sorry I can't answer to the phone right now but if you leave your name and number, I'll call you as soon as I can.

'Mummy.' Tears of relief spring into her eyes and she heaves breaths.

'Mummy? I'm sorry. Baby's…' She hiccoughs, unable to say. 'And Rachel's present… I took Baby for a walk and…'

A noise from the bedroom, like a person moving on the bed. Getting off a bed. A grunt.

'Mummy, can you come and get me now?' she says quickly.

The TV switches off. Silence. She puts the phone down quietly, slowly, and runs on her toes to the couch. Her thumb in her mouth, her eyes closed, she pretends to be asleep.

He stumbles in the bedroom. Runs into something. Swears.

The door opens the rest of the way.

'Where are you?' He flicks on the light.

Bree-Anna breathes even and deep, like people do when they sleep.

He moves closer, stands over her. 'You sleeping?'

Her heart thumps like a drum but she breathes steadily, pretending.

He grabs her wrist and yanks her up. Her arm might pop out of her shoulder, he yanks so hard, but she flops like a person waking and lets him drag her across the room, through the bedroom door, and lets him drop her against the bed.

He leaves the room, locking the door behind him.

Eloise locks up the pub and climbs into her car, another day over, exhaustion and aching feet. Bree-Anna's chubby freckled cheeks grin at her from the posters on the passenger seat.

She'll take them tomorrow, to town, to the train station perhaps—that's close to where she has to pick up her prints, and lots of people go through the station. Where else? The posters begin to feel like a millstone, as if by leaving them unseen she is directly responsible for preventing Bree-Anna from being found.

The car turns over on the third try, old bomb, but it will be a while, with uni fees (hopefully, portfolio submitted and accepted) and what not, before she can afford a new one.

And she has to clean Randall's place tomorrow. She hates setting foot in that dark old house, smelling like long-dead old lady and egg farts. Can she get out of it? Unlikely—none of the other cleaners will go near the place. He's scared them off with his creepy stuttering and staring eyes. She remembers him as a puny kid from primary school, a weird loner in high school. Perhaps that's why he doesn't scare her. He has the social skills of a worm. He always had the social skills of worm. He is just a worm. Worms are not dangerous. Just ugly and unable to cope with daylight.

She pulls onto the highway, her phone rings, probably Mike. No one else would ring this late. Still seething, feeling like a pawn in his spousal games, she ignores it. Will he ever let her take a portrait of him? Will they let her extend the deadline beyond the end of the month? If not, she has to wait another year. She couldn't bear waiting another year.

Damn it, she forgot to call Amber's mum. Too late now. Probably she's with Amber now. How could she keep away?

Eloise always got on with Amber's mother. After Eloise dropped out of Law and came home, it was Amber's mother who told her she ought to follow her heart, while her father looked at her with eyes that said he thought she was another of his failures, just like Anthony was proving to be at the time. Amber's mum suggested she ask Amber if she had any work, to tide her over until she found her feet. She was proud of Amber, Eloise could see, making the most of what had happened. Using Declan to meet the mums around the place that needed a cleaner. Building a reputation, having actual employees. Amber offered her a job. Eloise thought she might get her to do the paperwork or something, but she ended up cleaning for creeps like Colin, and stuck-up bureaucrats with babies in day care, who should be at home with their mothers if their mothers could drag themselves away from their high-heeled careers. Too many years of that and the pub until she got the courage and the money to buy better and better cameras, the right software, and do the thing she should have done all along. Followed her heart into photography. Hoping it wasn't too late. That she wasn't too old. Hadn't missed the boat.

Maybe she could take her camera to Randall's. Use him for the character study. That would really freak him out. She might even enjoy seeing him blush and stutter.

The petrol light flashes yellow. More money out of her

pocket. She can put forty bucks in and still have enough money for the prints.

The young fella at the petrol station recognises her. He's a busy-body gossip, always knows who's who, and what's what behind everyone's back. Forget hairdressers and barmaids, this guy is an attention-seeking freak who can't keep his lips zipped.

'Hey, how about Amber's kid?'

'Yeah,' Eloise says, ready for the same conversation she's had all day.

'You been to see her? How is she?'

'She's not good.'

'I seen the guy who took her.'

Eloise keys her PIN into the machine. 'Is that right?' He's so full of shit.

'Yeah, he came in and got petrol. The police took the CCTV footage, they're lookin' for him now. The cops have been in and out of here all day.'

'How do you know it was him?' Eloise puts her purse back into her bag.

'He said something, when he paid for the petrol, about seeing her. He was a rough lookin' guy. Looked like he hadn't slept in a year.'

'Those insomniacs, you can't trust 'em,' Eloise says.

'Yeah, I know, right?' He puts his elbows on the counter. 'I'm the one who found the toy stroller too. On the highway. I heard it on the radio and later I went out and had a ciggie and I saw it there. I didn't touch it. Fingerprints.'

'Fingerprints,' echoes Eloise, the machine finally telling her the transaction is approved.

'You need a receipt?' he asks, tearing the paper off.

She shakes her head, and he presses the no button. 'Anyhow,' he says, 'probably too late. He'd have done away with her by now, I figure.'

Eloise remembers Amber's frozen eyes, her distracted waiting for the phone to ring.

She should really call Amber's mum. First thing in the morning.

Approaching her house, the kitchen light is still on. Eloise's heart skips with panic. Her mother meets her at the door. 'You didn't answer your phone.'

'What? What's happened?' Eloise dumps her bag and keys and steps into the lounge, where a bomb has gone off. 'Where is he?' Her mother's hands shake, Eloise grabs them with her own and holds them steady. 'Did he hurt you?' Her mother shakes her head, her eyes brimming with tears. Eloise leads her to the couch, through the crunch of something broken, the remnants of a yellow vase, circa 1930 that used to be her grandmother's. So much for family heirlooms, dropping like flies.

Seated, her mother yanks her hands away and rubs her wrists.

'What happened? Is he still here?'

'He's settled down. He's sleeping, I think. I don't know. He hasn't made any noise for a while.' She rubs her hands over her face, and the skins moves loose and saggy under her palms. 'You should have answered the phone.'

'I was driving,' Eloise says. 'Besides, that was only just now, this happened a while ago. If he's in bed asleep—right?'

'I waited till the end of your shift. I don't want you to miss work.'

'Mum, I told you—ring me. Mike will be all right. I told him what's going on. He knows family comes first.' The irony of this declaration is not lost on Eloise.

'Oh.' Her mother's hands fall into her lap. 'I wish you wouldn't tell people.'

'He's got a disease, it's nothing to be ashamed of. People are going to find out. *People* might be able to help. What was it this time?'

Her mother exhales a huge breath and drops deep into the couch, almost disappearing into the cushions. 'We went out this morning, early.'

'Before I got up.'

'Yeah, he wanted papers and to go to the hardware store. I didn't want him to go on his own. He seemed so... vague. Like he gets. He even laughed about it. I said I wanted to go to Woolworth's, so he'd take me without complaining. He seemed all right after that. You know, he remembered what we went to town for. He was his old self. Then...' She groans and rubs her temples.

'Then?' Eloise prods.

'Oh, Eloise.' Her mother leans forward and over into her knees, folded over like she is in pain. 'It was so embarrassing. He thought the car was stolen. He was yelling at me. In front of everyone—oh god! He accused me of leaving it unlocked. The car was right there, Eloise, in front of us. He was looking for the blue Ford. The one we sold—what, nine years ago!'

'You didn't say anything when you got home. I wouldn't have gone to work if you'd have told me. You have to tell me.'

'You've enough to worry about. Amber to visit. That poor little girl. How is Amber? When I think...'

'You are more important than Amber. You have to tell me when stuff happens. No matter what.'

'Well, he was over it by then. A bit grumpy. You saw he was a bit grumpy, but I made him some lunch and he looked at the papers. I don't know if he knows what he reads anymore, but he looked at the papers, tinkered about in the shed. I hid the car keys—in case he decided to go off like last time.'

Eloise reaches for her mother's shoulder, rubs it gently. 'He's getting worse, isn't he?'

Her mother nods her head, tears on her cheeks. 'I don't know how much longer I can do this for.'

'We have to get him back to the doctor.'

'He won't go.'

'Have you tried?'

'Of course, I've tried. Eloise, he's too young for this. It's not fair. This was supposed to be our time. To see the Kimberleys, the Reef, Venice, Paris. Wander wherever the fancy took us.' She laughs. 'Can you imagine?'

'No, I can't.' Eloise remains sombre, tired, footsore. 'What happened to...' She waves her hand, indicating the chaos in the room, the half-toppled Christmas tree.

'I don't know. I was cooking dinner. Roast pork. I left some for you.'

'I said not to make me dinner.'

'Yeah, well, no one else ate it. I can't eat. Your father—he makes me so angry. I know I shouldn't get angry. It's not his fault, but... I cooked all that food. He loves roast pork.'

'This is not about the pork though, is it?'

'Who the hell knows. He just got... weird... shuffling around, he didn't seem able to speak. I tried to get him in a chair, calm him down, put on the TV. He just got more... belligerent—like a two-year-old. I got him sitting down. He covered his ears,' she covers her own ears, 'and moaned until I turned the TV down. Almost to no sound at all. When I went to get him for dinner, he was asleep. I left him there—it was easier.' She sighs. 'Then I got guilty. I thought I should wake him—before you got home, get him into bed. Like a normal person. He just went berserk. Eloise, he didn't recognise me!' She stabs herself in the chest with her finger. 'That's never happened before—he thought I was an intruder. He kept calling for Anthony. I thought he was going to hit me! He's not a violent man. He never was a violent man. But I thought... So I went to your room and closed the door. He trashed the place, disappeared into the bedroom and I don't know what. That was when I came out, rang you.'

'You should have taken the phone with you, rung the police.'

Her mother looks at her, indignant. 'I couldn't do *that* to him.'

'Mum.' Eloise sighs and moves closer, hugging the stiff, resistant body of her mother. She gives up, and looking directly at her mother, says, 'We will get him to the doctor. There might be some medication. To settle him down. You have to feel safe in your own home.'

Her mother nods. 'Something to dope the dope up would make my day.'

Eloise laughs. 'That's terrible!'

Her mother stands, wobbling, a decade or two older than she should be. 'I'm sorry, I didn't mean it. I'm so tired. I'm going to sleep in Anthony's... in the spare room. Will you...'

Eloise rises and steers her mother with her hand on her back. 'I'll clear up, sleep on the couch. Make sure he doesn't wander off again.'

'Lock the door,' her mother says, urgency in her voice.

'I'll lock the door,' she replies and watches her mother sway down the dark hallway.

Eloise sweeps up the broken glass, rights the wrongs in the room to normalcy. She will never get away from here. This will be her purgatory. She should have gone to Sydney and become a junkie like Anthony. No one expected anything of Anthony. She thinks these things and at the same time hates herself for thinking them. It is not about her. It is about her mum and her dad, him turning into a demented old man before his time and her mother bearing the brunt of caring for him. Still, the resentment of pushing her dreams aside boils within her. How can she do both? Leave and stay. She can't.

What if Anthony isn't lying? What if he really has gone straight this time?

What if this is the last chance her father has of seeing Anthony and actually remembering him?

She grabs a blanket, though she's not cold, wraps herself into a ball on the couch, skims through the home phone to the last recorded received call.

She takes a deep breath and dials the number.

TUESDAY

Bree-Anna wakes, her tummy proper hungry without the sick at the same time. She slept on the floor, pushed up tight in her new hiding place between the wall and the dresser. Her mum will get up, make her coffee, take it and her first cigarette onto the patio, and listen to her messages. She has a coffee and ciggie every morning. Maybe she will have a second coffee and another cigarette and *then* she will come. She has to come.

She lifts up her nightie and touches the bluing bruise on her thigh. She owes him forever. Her shoulders are sore from where they squashed between the wall and the dresser. The back of her head still hurts when she touches it. She slides out of her hidey-hole and across the prickling carpet. She glances at the bed and her stomach dances a little to find it empty. She rises slowly to her feet and stumbles to the window.

The outside world is pink and soft. The car park is empty. Absolutely empty. Not a single car. It must be early. She grasps the windowsill, scraping the peeling the paint off with her fingernails. A dog barks in the distance. *Ruff, ruff, ruff.* The birds muck about singing and screeching. It's too early for the shops to open. She will have to wait a little while. Mummy never gets up this early.

A familiar tug in her belly tells her she must wee. The chamber pot stinks. She used it yesterday, in the afternoon, and now she has to use it again. When she drags it from under the chair, wee splashes up its sides and onto the carpet. She looks behind her shoulder to the door, but she can't hear him, and the door knob doesn't turn.

Weeing into the cold pot, yesterday's pee spurts up onto her bare bum and it is not nice. Bree-Anna tries to make her new wee fall more gently, but it is impossible. When she's done, she wishes for toilet paper. Wishing for it gets nothing.

Food, food, food. If she was at home, she would eat a ginormous bowl of Coco Pops with cold, cold milk. Then she would have toast with jam. Her tummy rumbles. Even better would be her favourite breakfast of all time. The one Grandma makes. Hash browns and bacon and baked beans and sausages. Pork sausages from the butcher, not the supermarket. Grandma has a runny fried egg with hers. Declan has hard fried. Declan says eggs from Grandma's chickens are more yellow and more tasty. But Bree-Anna doesn't like eggs so she wouldn't know. Grandma used to give Mummy cartons of eggs to take home but they stayed in the fridge and didn't get cooked at all.

She misses Grandma's old house. It used to be a farm house, but the farmer built a new house with bricks and sold the old wooden one to Grandma. Her Grandpa used to live there and grow vegetables, but he died before Bree-Anna was born and now there is just Grandma and chickens and puppies and cats. One of the best things about visiting Grandma—other than feeding the chickens and collecting the eggs, which might be more better if she liked eggs, or the chickens didn't poo on you when you picked them up—was the dogs. When people go on holidays, Grandma looks after their dogs for them. She says people like it because she doesn't put the dogs in cages like the kennels do. But she charges more and hopes the council mans don't ever find out because she doesn't really have all the proper permissions.

Grandma's special dogs that are hers are Maltese; they are dogs with papers and she can sell their puppies for millions of dollars. Zach and Toby are the boys and Fergie and Diana are the girls. It is lots of dogs to have in the house. They run up and down the hallway and slip on the wood floors and it is like they are fighting, but that is how dogs play. Fergie is her favourite because she knowed her from when she was a puppy. Bree-Anna always tries to get her to sleep on her bed with her but she gets up in the night and scratches on the door and Bree-Anna has to get up and let her out so she can get into bed with Grandma and Diana and Toby and Zach.

Whenever Mummy walks in the house she says, 'It smells like dog in here,' and crinkles her nose. Bree-Anna likes the smell, it makes her think of clean dirt and the tickle of fur on her face.

Fergie's three puppies slept so still. Bree-Anna stroked their backs just to see them twitch, so she knew they were still alive. When they woke up, they wriggled around like slugs because they couldn't see where they were going. Her favourite was Fatty. Grandma called him that because he always got to Fergie's boobies first and stayed the longest and weighed a whole one hundred more than the other two puppies.

Grandma said she could have Fatty. When he was older and allowed to leave Fergie.

Mummy said no.

Bree-Anna said pleeeaase and even got on her knees.

Her mother walked around her and said no.

Grandma said, let the girl have a dog.

Mummy said, you shouldn't have got her hopes up.

Her hopes were up.

She picked up Fatty, and Fergie followed her because she didn't like it when you took her puppies. She pressed Fatty to her cheek and said, look Mummy he's so sweet and soft.

Mummy groaned and turned away and said, Where's Declan?

Bree-Anna shuffled around in front of her. Just look, Mummy, and she held him up for her to see closer. Touch him.

Mummy spun around to Grandma, What the hell do you think you're doing putting a dog in her head? I said last time, and the time before. I do not want a dog. I don't have time to walk a dog. I don't have time to feed a dog. I don't want a dog.

Grandma said, Sometimes it's not about what you want, Amber.

What is that supposed to mean? Mummy stomped over and took Fatty off her and almost threw him back with the other two puppies.

Careful, Mummy, you'll hurt him.

Amber! Grandma said.

Bree-Anna knelt down and ran her finger over his silk fur and thought, yeah, sometimes it is about what I want. But she didn't say it. Instead she said, there there, Fatty. Fergie came back and huddled over them like a good mummy.

Oh, for god's sake, Bree-Anna, get up and get your things. I don't have time for this.

You don't have time for this! Grandma said. You drop them off on Thursday and say you will pick them up on Saturday and without a word you leave them here till today. What have you been doing? Gallivanting about the place with some deadbeat man? I hope you used some birth control because you sure as hell ain't got enough time for the kids you got. What was I thinking, letting you have responsibility for a dog? You never cared for anything properly in your life.

Grandma's face was all red and her hands shook when she wiped the hair out her eyes.

Mummy walked right up close to Grandma and Bree-Anna thought she was going to kiss her cheek but instead she said, you self-righteous bitch. Then she grabbed her handbag and called out, we're leaving.

Bree-Anna scrambled to her feet. Mummy came and grabbed her arm and yanked her out the door, calling loud to Declan. Bree-Anna twisted back and saw Grandma, her face wet with tears, reaching out to hug her goodbye, but Bree-Anna wasn't even able to get her bag let alone kiss Grandma goodbye. Lucky Declan brought out her bag when he came. He slammed the car door and wouldn't talk. Bree-Anna didn't know if he was angry about leaving in a hurry or because of Fatty. He wanted Fatty too.

Bree-Anna didn't want to take Fatty home anymore. The sadness of the fight made her want nothing nice ever again.

That was before she got Baby. Baby came in the mail on her birthday and she never got to see the card but she knew Grandma posted it even though she could have brought her over herself. Except she wasn't allowed to step foot in this house ever again!

Sometimes Bree-Anna wondered if having Baby was as good as having Fatty would be. If Fatty was big and tough, he might have bit Mr Randall instead of getting put in a suitcase. But Fatty was only going to grow up to be little and fluffy and white so Mr Randall wouldn't have been scared of him.

Outside the window, in the car park, a car arrives and drives all the way around the back where the sign says: No Customer Entry. A bit later a man comes and unlocks the newsagent's roller door. The door stays half open for a while until another car comes and a fat man wearing a suit jogs wobbling funny to the door and calls under it. She has a funny feeling about her photo in the paper. Why did they do that? The newsagent man comes and opens the roller door the rest of the way. After the man leaves with his newspaper, the store man pulls out all the displays with books and toys and Christmas decorations to sell. Mummy calls it *desperation in the age of online news.* She says it's all overpriced and can't compete with the cheap shop and their made-in-China trash. But Mummy cleans for Mrs Newsman and so she always buys magazines there and bought Bree-Anna a book that time.

More cars come. People mill outside Woolworth's until at last someone opens the doors and they go in. About now? Her mother would be waking. Or is it too early?

Her tummy growls at her. She could eat a horse. A horse, a pig, and a cow. Especially a pig made into bacon.

Prickles like pins scrape her back when she hears him at the door. She makes herself not turn. She makes herself keep watching the window.

The door creaks when it opens and she can feel him standing in the doorway, just standing there looking at her back, her back prickling with the stare from his eyes. It is like when Declan comes and stands in her bedroom doorway just to bug her. If she throws something at Declan or swears at him, he gets what he wants because she is being a fish. If she ignores him, he comes and bugs more, he pokes her, tries to steal Baby, calls her a slob, until she gives in and becomes an angry fish. One time, because she was bored and it was raining, she said to Declan, *Wanna play snakes and ladders?* And that is what they did. No teasing. Sometimes pretending to be nice, even when you don't feel like being nice, makes other people nice.

She turns and smiles. 'Good morning, Mr Randall.' He takes a step back, looks like he might turn and leave again, shakes his head, blinks his eyes and says, 'Well, about time you grew some manners, young lady.'

He crosses the room toward her. 'What stinks?' She looks over at the chamber pot. 'Oh, you done potty, little baby.' She cringes because she is not a baby, but she smiles and says yes.

'Well, don't just leave it there! Tip it out the window.'

She glances back at the window and the filling up car park beyond it. 'I don't know how it opens.'

'Stupid bitch.' He pushes her out of the way. 'Watch,' he says, his tangled eyebrows lifting high above his eyes.

She watches. First, he unlatches something above the bottom half of the window. Then he pushes it up with his hands on the pane. Then, holding it there, he pulls out little metal holders from each side of the window and lets the window rest on them.

'Simple,' he says. 'Even a baby could do it. Now, tip it out.'

Bree-Anna walks careful so as not to spill wee on the carpet. She leans far out the window and tips.

He leans over her and sniffs. 'You got some on the house,' he growls in her ear, and lifts her legs and shoves her head out the window. Bree-Anna screams, grabs at air, slips, her chest hanging out, the windowsill digging into her belly. She presses her hands against the outside of the house and pants. The ground is far below.

'Look! Do you see?'

'Yes,' she screeches.

He pulls at her hips and scrapes her almost back in, holds her aloft and puts his cheek close to hers. 'If your mother doesn't come, I'll have to bury you down there,' he says, polite as pie.

She nods.

'You know she's not coming, right?'

But she is coming. Bree-Anna knows because she rang her and left a message. She always comes. At long last, she always comes.

Like magic, there is a knock on the door. 'Mummy!' Bree-Anna runs for the door, happy, happy dancing through it. He catches her, wraps his arm around her, and shoves his hand over her mouth. She kicks and worms to get out of his grasp, but he holds tighter and crunches her bones together. She squirms harder, tries to get her teeth into his hand.

The knock comes again, and he says, 'What the fuck?' He drags her toward the dresser, her feet scraping across the carpet. She pushes to get to her feet. He lets go of her mouth and she lets out a squeal. He bangs her head on the dresser and hisses, 'Shut up.' He opens a drawer. She feels a trickle of blood on her forehead. Mummy is gonna be so mad with him when she sees her bleeding head. She pants and says *Mummy,* her voice croaking, and he stuffs something in her mouth—a sock, it smells of dirty feet and presses on the back of her throat, and she gags. She wiggles and squirms and kicks, wants to get him where it hurts again. Twists to find that place.

'Colin,' a voice calls from the front door.

'Yeah,' he shouts back. 'Coming.'

Then, of all the strange things to have in his pocket, he gets a roll of red tape. Throwing her to the ground, he sits on her chest, holds her wrists together with one hand, finds the end of the tape with his mouth, and with his other hand winds it around and around her wrist. Rips the end off with his teeth. She wriggles and twists beneath him. Vomit gags at the back of her throat and she pants through her nose, trying to breathe.

Her hands pressed together, he twists around and does the same to her feet. Then he picks her up in his arms. Looks around, spinning in a circle.

'Colin!' Banging on the door.

Mummy, Mummy, Mummy, Bree-Anna thinks—*just come in, break down the door*. Her heart is racing and racing and she will choke to death.

He opens the wardrobe door and rolls her into it, stuffs her legs in last, and leans his head in the dark with her so that his eyes pop white in the dark. 'Make a fuckin' noise and I'll kill ya. Dead forever,' he says and closes the wardrobe door. She hears him drag something over in front of the wardrobe door.

In the dark wardrobe, dead people's clothes hang over her, shoes dig into her, and from the top of the wardrobe she can hear Baby, blaming her for this mess. Tears run down her cheeks and she can't move to wipe them away.

Eloise parks behind the absurd green station wagon Colin's mother drove before she died and Colin now slinks around town in. Was there ever a more stupid coloured car? Lucky he doesn't go around doing crimes; he would stand out like a sore thumb.

At the top of the stairs, she calls out, knocks, and pushes on the door. Locked! He doesn't usually lock the door. He had better be home; she hasn't time to wait for him. The car is here, she reassures herself. Colin never walks anywhere, not even not ever next door to the shops, which must be all of a few hundred metres.

She bangs her fist on the door and calls again. He shouts back. *Damn you, Colin*, she thinks to herself. She can hear him banging around doing some darned thing. She's got places to be, people to see, things to do. She can't afford to stand around on the hot stairs waiting for him to hide his wanking magazines or whatever the hell he's doing. She punches the door again. 'Colin!' she shouts.

When he finally thrusts the door open, he stands in the doorway, more agitated than usual. 'W-w-w-what are you doing here?' he stutters, looks down at his feet and cracks his knuckles. Such a foul habit. Something teenagers do and grow out of. Not Colin.

'Come to clean, Colin, like I always do on Tuesdays.' She pushes past him.

He follows her to the stinking pig-sty kitchen—egg shells and egg cartons, dirty plates. 'I d-don't w-want you here,' he says from behind her.

'Yeah, well, if I don't clean this shit up, you'll probably get rats and catch the plague and die.' No great loss. 'We wouldn't want that, would we?' She starts clearing up the bench-top; he flutters about in the doorway watching. No wonder the other cleaners won't come. Being watched with his jittery intensity is like being held under a microscope by a scientist with Parkinson's disease. Still, he seems worse than usual.

'What's the matter, Colin, ants in your pants?'

He grunts and disappears out of the room. Thank you, god. Eloise raises her chin to the heavens. With efficiency she transforms the kitchen into something near to habitable and shifts into the bathroom. Damn the idea of mopping today. He won't even notice if she doesn't do it. The bathroom stinks of stale piss and rot. She gulps a breath and lifts the lid on the dirty clothes basket.

'Colin, you haven't done the washing again. I'm not your slave, you know.' She shoves the basket along the ground with her foot. He meets her, blocking her way down the hall. 'I'll put them in machine for you, but you'll have to hang them out yourself.'

He kicks at the basket with his feet.

'Colin? You hear me?'

'Yeah,' he says. 'Use the f-front stairs—the back ones a… aren't g-good.'

'Aren't good? Whatever.' She shakes her head and drags the basket along the ground, hefts it down the front stairs and under the house to the laundry. Useless piece of shit. You'd think he could at least wash a load of clothes in a week. She opens the machine to find a clump of wet clothes. The ones she put in the machine last week. 'I'm not paid to do this,' she calls through the floor boards. Twit. 'If you want me to do the washing, you got to pay more.' She dumps the dirty clothes on top of the wet clothes. Something pink slides into the machine. That's odd. Maybe Colin got himself a girlfriend. Unlikely. It all stinks of piss. What's he been doing? Pissing his pants? She pours in extra detergent and bangs down the lid. 'I don't get paid to do this,' she calls up again, though he can't hear her.

She stomps up the stairs, looks at her watch. She's not giving him any more than another twenty-five minutes—no matter what else needs to be done. She's got to have a word with Amber. When Amber is ready to have a word. If Amber is ever ready to have a word. Amber needs to talk to the solicitor guy who pays the bills. Get another hour out of him. There is more here than she can do in the time she's got.

At the top of the stairs she shouts, 'Don't forget to hang it out!' She heads back to the mouldy shit-house bathroom and gives in, sweeping and mopping both rooms and then with ten minutes to spare goes to the loungeroom.

'I've only got ten minutes left, you want me to dust or vacuum? I don't have time for both. I got other things to do today and you only pay for an hour.' She decides to dust because it's easier than wrangling the old vacuum out of the hall cupboard. 'You need another hour. You should talk to your man about buying another hour. Can you afford another hour?'

He sits on the couch, his feet planted on the floor. 'I got m-more m-money than y-you,' he replies.

'Yeah, well, that wouldn't be too hard.' She's got even less after her talking to Anthony last night. She grabs a dust cloth from the hall cupboard and returns to the room. Most houses she cleans when no one is home. They are at work and she can nose around and do things as she likes. Colin pulls his legs up off the floor, his knees all out at angles, but he doesn't look at her.

'It'll be Christmas soon,' she says, wiping down the coffee table. 'What are you doing Christmas day? Is your sister coming? Are you going to hers?'

He doesn't answer. She turns to the wall. An empty gap screams no TV. 'Where's the TV? Is it broken? They don't make anything to last these days.' She dusts around where the TV should be and moves into Colin's room, does a cursory dust—he won't even notice what she's missed. Glances at her watch again. Five minutes.

The last room is his mother's old room. No one uses it so it is easy. Colin's disappeared. She touches the door handle and turns the knob. Opens the door.

He jumps in front of her and bars her way. 'Don't go in there.' He looks her right in the eye, his eyelids twitching.

She looks past him. He's taken up sleeping in his mother's room. The bed is ruffled and there's crap all over the floor. She sighs. She's definitely going to ask for more money if she has to clean up this mess every week.

'It's a pig-sty, Colin.' And it smells like piss. He is pissing his pants. Or pissing out the window? There's a damp patch on the carpet… surely not. She presses her shoulder against him to get by and he pushes back.

'I t-t-told A-a-amber to t-t-tell you n-not to come.'

Eloise raises her eyebrows at him. He gets weirder by the minute. She puts her hand on her hip and leans on the door-frame. 'Well, she never told me. She's probably got other things on her mind.'

'Like w-what?'

'Like Bree-Anna. Her daughter.'

'Huh?' He grins through his ugly little short teeth, looking like he still has his baby teeth.

'She's missing.' Eloise rises on her toes to see beyond his shoulder into the bedroom. The TV is in there. 'Since Sunday.'

'She l-lost her?' He kicks his feet on the carpet.

'Probably some nutter snatched her. From the highway. They found her toy stroller there. Amber's frantic with worry. Everyone thinks the kid is dead.' Eloise regrets her candour. A noise comes from the cupboard. Does he have rats? One day when she is a rich and famous travel photographer, she won't have to clean up other people's grossness and she'll be able to laugh about Colin's piss-smelling, rat-infested house.

Colin grabs her arm and drags her through the door. 'You c-can g-go now.'

Shit! He's never touched her before. She shakes him off. The things she has to put up with. Whatever, she's got other things to do. 'Whatever you say. You're paying.'

She slams the door behind her and runs down the stairs. At the bottom, she grits her teeth. 'Merry Christmas to you too, Colin. I'm sure Santa will bring you something good. Not.'

Bree-Anna twists and turns in the tiny wardrobe. She bangs against the wardrobe walls with her elbows and knees, her chest heaving for air. All this time he has been lying to her. Mummy doesn't know she is here. People think she is dead!

She can't hear them talking anymore. Are they still there? She moans through her gagged mouth, kicks and bucks; junk falls and tumbles around her. A racket—she's got to make a racket.

Mummy doesn't know she is here. Mummy is frantic with worry. For her. Eloise came to clean, even though he said not to, and she said it. People think she is dead. No one is coming for her. Declan can't ring Grandma. Grandma can't come. Her father doesn't know she is born. He isn't coming. No one is coming.

Everyone thinks she is dead. She is not dead. Eloise *must* hear her.

A thump on the wardrobe door startles her. She stills, her breathing heavy.

'Shut the fuck up.' He says every word in a slow whisper, just on the other side of the door. 'She's gone. She can't hear you. No one can hear you.'

She groans and thrashes anyway. He bangs on the door again. 'You want me to kill you now?' he shouts. 'Right now?'

She stops. Squeezes her eyes closed. Tears burn down her face, wet like she has been in the bath. Snot streams out of her nose. She sniffs. She can't breathe. Snot and sock.

He smacks the door again and it bends in on her and splits, a closed crack. He's kicking it again and again. Bree-Anna hides her face in her elbows; the door snaps and spits splinters at her. She begs in strangled moans for him to stop until the door falls lopsided, hanging from one hinge.

Through the gap she can see him, his fists clenched, stamping the floor like a boy having a tantrum.

He stops. His eyes meet hers and he steps forward, and Bree-Anna squeezes back into the cupboard though she can't move any deeper.

'Do you think she suspected anything?' He spins away and shakes his hands and turns back. 'Man, I almost died when she opened the door. I was thinking, don't clean Mum's room this week. Don't clean Mum's room this week. And damn, she opens the door, just like that.' He takes another step forward and leans down, points at his head with his gnarled long finger. 'But

I thought quick. I was right there saying, Don't go in there. Don't go in there. Did you hear me?'

Bree-Anna nods. She heard him.

He stands up again and turns to the window. 'We make a good team! But…' He spins back toward her. 'Why you got to go and make all that noise? Do you think she heard you?'

He walks out of her sight and back in, back and forth, she counts. Six times his feet and knees come into view. Snot runs from her nose, tears hot in her eyes.

'What are we going to do? What? What? What?' And he's on his hands and knees, looking in at her again.

She shakes her head.

He stands and paces again. 'We could say I found you wandering in the bush. Like we said yesterday. We shoulda done it yesterday. Is today too late?' He pulls the hanging cupboard door away and crashes it against the bed. He grabs her tied together ankles, digs his nails into her calves. 'Is today too late?'

She shakes her head.

'You think it's not too late? Do you think I would get the reward?' He stands up again. 'Is there a reward?' Then he laughs and throws his hands in the air. 'I don't need the reward. I got money. No, no, this is for Amber.' He looks back at her. 'Remember, dinner at the pub and then back to your place.' He thrusts his hips at her and laughs.

'There is just one problem.' He gets down and shuffles on his knees toward her and buries his head in the cupboard with her. 'The problem is, can I trust you?'

She nods her head. Yes, yes. She wants to say yes.

'You would have to lie. Lie and say you were wandering in the bush, lost and scared, and then wow! Hero! Colin Randall turns up and saves the day!'

She nods and sniffs. Yes. She could do that.

His eyes shine white and wide, the only brightness in the cupboard. She tries to sniff snot back into her nose and chokes. He takes the sock out of her mouth. She gasps in air and lets saliva flow into her cotton-wool mouth.

'Tell me, bitch, about being lost in the bush.'

She hiccoughs and sniffles. Her dry mouth stuck together, the words stuck in her throat, not even in her head.

'Ahh!' He punches the cupboard and winces with pain, pulling his head out of the darkness and back into the room. 'Bitch.' He holds his hand in his lap. 'I think you broke my hand.' He rocks back and forth.

'I can't trust you at all. Look at all you done to me. Kicked me in the balls! Ball breaker. Refuse to eat the food I bring ya. Hides.' He gestures around the room. 'Hides from me all the time.' He clutches his hands together again. 'No, first chance you get, you gonna tell them…' His teeth come together and he spits through them. 'You can't do what you're told.'

He drops cross-legged in front of the cupboard door. 'The way I see it, we got two options. I kill ya or you die.'

Bree-Anna shakes her head. Takes a deep breath and finds her voice. 'I can lie.' She can barely hear herself. 'I can. I can.'

'You ever lied before?' He raised his eyebrow.

She nods her head.

'Then,' he grins, 'how do I know you're not lying now?'

She shakes her head and squeaks, 'No.'

He sighs. 'I gotta think about it.' He lies back, his legs still crossed, his knees in the air. Hairs poking out of his pants.

Bree-Anna closes her eyes. Please, please she prays. She can lie. She really can. She really will lie. She can make up the biggest story about going to Rachel's and going the wrong way and sleeping under trees and getting wet in the rain. She can make up stories if she has to. They can make the story up together.

He sits up suddenly, flinging himself up off the ground and says, 'How long does it take to starve to death?'

Bree-Anna shakes her head and sniffles.

'I think,' he says, 'you die of thirst first. I think I saw that on TV. Cause if you die of thirst, I can just take you out there in the bush and no one ain't ever gonna ask me anything about it. What do you think?'

She moves her head from side to side. No. She shudders and shrinks tighter into the cupboard.

'But what if they come looking for you? If that bitch heard you kicking? What did you kick and make that noise for?'

A hard ball of fear in her stomach rises up into Bree-Anna's mouth. She tries to swallow, her throat dry and furry and she can't breathe any air in. She's forgotten how to breathe and she pants, trying to fill her empty chest.

'Making noise spoils everything. You realise I could go to jail for what I done? You thought of that? You even care?' He thrusts his face into hers. 'You listening to me?'

He seizes her ankles. Yanks. Her legs jerk and her back scrapes out and over and bumps onto the floor.

Her nightie is up, around her waist. He can see what she's got. She wants to pull it down, she can't. She pants deep empty breaths of air.

'Fuckin' fuck fuck,' he shouts.

She writhes, groaning and panting. Cover herself. Don't let him see what she's got.

The first kick gets her in the stomach. Knocks the last wind out of her. She brings her knees up over the pain. Pulls her face between her elbows. He kicks her again. In her back.

The next kick smashes the back of her head. Then there is black.

First, Eloise heads into town. There's a mix of excitement and fear about picking up her prints. Will they be good enough? She never really knows how they will look. She can see them on the computer screen, print them off, but when they are printed properly, they come to life or they disappoint. They have to be good enough for the portfolio or... or what? What is her plan B if she doesn't get in?

People shopping—full of Christmas cheer and Christmas cash. Or credit. Credit more likely. She picks up some nice perfume she knows her mum likes and some chocolate-coated almonds her dad likes. If he remembers he likes them. Can you forget something like that or is it just part of you? Like an innate preference.

The shopping centre management takes some of Bree-Anna's posters for the noticeboard and say they will put some in the toilets too. They are very accommodating and nod grimly when they look at her photocopy of Bree-Anna's freckled head.

Last of all, she opens the sliding door of the Kodak shop. The old guy recognises her and has her prints on the counter before she is inside. So he should, she spends enough money here.

'They turned out pretty good,' he says.

She smiles, wondering what gives him the right to even look at them, isn't that like a privacy thing? 'How much?' she says, and doesn't give him the satisfaction of looking at them.

In her baking car, she slides the enlargements out of the envelope, holding her breath. The sky blares blue against the grey of the dead tree trunk. Derivative, dull. Oh, god, she can't even look at the rest. She throws the package on the passenger seat. Maybe they will be better when she puts them together with the others.

She has her familiar sinking feeling of imminent failure, of stuckness, of never being good enough. She pushes it back and away. *Just get on with it*, she thinks.

She checks her phone—Mike still hasn't replied to her text. How much effort does it take to reply? Should she ring? He said maybe today. She shuffles the phone around and around in her hand. A man squeezes past her car, dragging a kid behind him. The kid looks in at her, ice-cream smeared around its face.

She rings her mum instead.

'Hi Mum, how is Dad?'

'He's doing fine. Better than yesterday.'

'You talk to him about the doctor?'

'Not yet.'

'You want me to do it?'

'No, no. Don't you worry. I'll work it out. After Christmas. Let's get through Christmas.'

After Christmas. Is she joking? She sighs. 'Okay, I'll be home soon.'

'Are you going to see Amber?'

'I wasn't going to. Why? Has something happened?'

'You should go see her. Who else has she got?'

A string of one-night stands?

'Her mum?'

'Have they made up?'

'God, they should do. Why wouldn't they in these circumstances?'

'You know Amber. Pig-headed. You should check on her.'

'All right.'

She swings the car out of the car park, the steering wheel burning in her hand, the air-con blasting with inefficiency. Some cranky woman in a four-wheel-drive gives her the evil eye. Eloise gives her the finger. Leaving this crap hole behind can't be a bad thing. She should go whether she gets into uni or not.

She listens to the news. Bree-Anna isn't in the news anymore. It's all about traffic fatalities and heat waves. Is the media's memory so short? How do they expect to find her? Well, they don't. Amber. Amber will be off her tree. She does feel sorry for her. She wouldn't wish this on anyone, not even Amber. Visiting Amber is the right thing to do.

She pulls up at Amber's house, checks for messages again. Nothing.

She knocks a warning, calls hello, and opens the door. The cop is gone. She smiles at Declan sitting on the couch, his game on his lap, but he's not playing. Half those damn posters are still in her car. She meant to stop at the train station. She forgot. What is she supposed to do with them all? The Christmas tree in the corner has developed a lean. Dark and depressing.

'Hey Declan.' She kneels in front of him and rubs his knee. 'How you bearing up?'

He nods at her. Sort of.

'That cop not hanging around anymore?'

He shakes his head.

Amber turns up at the door and looks at her.

'Amber,' Eloise says.

Amber turns and shuffles away.

Eloise follows, her heart beating, her stomach turning. How dare she be worried about her portfolio, Mike, when Amber has this on her plate? Then again, when did Amber ever ask after her dad? All the time, if she is honest. Damn her.

'I bought some food,' Eloise says. 'Just some microwave dinners. Something you or Declan can just heat up when you're hungry.' She opens the fridge, frigid air churns out at her.

'It's stuffy in here.' She opens the back door and window over the sink. She leans against the sink. 'You heard anything?'

Amber twirls her coffee cup around and around on the table.

'Have you been talking to your mum? Has she been over?'

'Don't stick your nose in, Eloise,' Amber sighs.

Eloise pulls up a chair and sits. Amber's mobile phone is on the table. 'You've got lots of messages—maybe you should listen to them.'

'Why?'

'Maybe... whoever...'

'They are just clients ringing. I can see who is ringing. It's called caller ID. I'm sure you've heard of it.'

'They might know something. They might not want to tell the police. Have the police told you anything?' Eloise asks.

'No. They said I should wait here. Fucking waiting is what I am doing.'

Amber looks at the phone, bites her lip, her heel tapping a rapid beat on the floor. 'Shit... do you think? I was just thinking, customers being busy bodies...' She drags the phone toward her. 'I can't...' she says and pushes the phone away.

Eloise picks up the phone. 'I'll do it. We'll put it on speaker.'

The first two messages are clients—saying they are thinking of Amber in this difficult time. That if she needs anything they should call. Like Bree-Anna is dead. Amber wraps her arms over her head and thumps her forehead on the table. Eloise deletes both messages.

Then there is Colin Randall. Stuttering away. Cancelling Eloise. Strange prick was telling the truth. Too late. She's been and gone.

Amber draws in a deep breath, her face buried in the table. 'Turn it off. The next one is Randall again. I saw it come through.'

The phone says, 'Message received at ten twenty-six on...'

'Hang up,' Amber says and snatches the phone back, presses the number five. 'Message deleted,' the phone replies and Amber hangs up. Her hand trembles. 'I told you it was a waste of time. Bree-Anna will ring on the landline.'

Amber looks up at Eloise. 'I'll kill myself if they don't find her.'

Everything throbs. Grey. Blur. Knife sharp pain in her head. Eyes can't stay open. Close to swirling colours. Her body pulses. *Boom boom*. Like a drum being smacked. *Boom boom. Boom boom*. In her ears. *Boom boom*.

Black again.

Boom boom.

Dumb-dumb.

Sorry, Baby. *Boom boom*. Baby. Baby. Don't call me dumb-dumb. I love you, Baby.

You made this mess. Dumb-dumb.

I know.

Get me out of this suitcase. I don't want to go on holiday with *him*. Take me home.

I can't take you home.

Take me home. It's time to go home.

I don't know how.

Dumb-dumb.

Footsteps. *Stomp stomp* around her. A toe in her stomach. Sharp nail. Rolling her. Jerking to her back and forth. Eyes flutter light to dark and in the blur. Is that... Can she see... Mummy? I can't wake up. There's no school today.

Hot. Sick.

Hot and sick. The troll came when she was hot and sick. He touched her forehead. You're burning up. Like fire, he said.

Grandma said, being scared makes you braver.

Grandma is a liar.

Puppy licks her face. Velvet fur on her face. Fatty fatty. How did he find her? It must mean she's dead.

Fire hot. You're burning up. A flame? She will catch fire. No, no. He touches her forehead. Smiles with crooked teeth. She didn't know he was a troll yet. He came in her bedroom. Where's Mummy?

Mummy's in bed still.

I feel sick.

You are sick. You're burning up.

Will I catch fire?

Oh, you hot. You gonna catch fire for sure.

Baby says, Forget it. Forget it. You should not try and remember. The troll's not even here.

I'm not trying to remember. I am just remembering. Because it's hot. Hot and sick.

Why'd we even leave? Why'd we go for that walk?

The party. Rachel's party.

And to get away from the troll. Because he was awake and Mummy was asleep. Just like last time.

Baby says, You should try and wake up. Wake up so we can go home. Take me home.

Home.

White blobs bob behind her eyes. Up and down. Like a see-saw. Her tummy rocks too. Like a boat. Sea sick. Baby, make it stop. A noise like a whine comes from her mouth. A kick in the stomach knocks the breath from her.

Can't breathe. Pull in air. Pull in air. Nothing. Nothing.

You love that dog more than me.

No, Baby.

The carpet scratches her skin. She wants to move her legs. To straighten them. To stretch the cramp in her thigh. She has to remind her brain how to make her leg move. Tell her body where her leg is. Near her hip. At the end of her hip. She shudders and her body remembers and her leg moves and pain burns through her, her ankles tied tight together. She forgot. Her wrists are tied too.

She's almost awake. Does she want to be awake?

Of course you want to be awake, Baby screams.

Don't scream, Baby, he will hear you. I'm going back to sleep. Sleep. It is easier when I am asleep.

Grandma lied when she said being scared makes you braver. She is more scared than she has ever been and she has no brave. Being dead would be easier than being brave.

The kids in the swimming pool squeal. The water laps her toes. The big pool. Always Grandma watched her in the little kids' pool. The warm kiddie pool water came up to her knees. But the big pool went over her head. Way over her head. It came up to Grandma's shoulders. Grandma held out her arms and said, Come on, I will look after you. I won't let you drown.

Chicken, Declan says and ducks under the water like an ugly boy dolphin.

Tears prick at her eyes. I'm not chicken. I'm scared.

Grandma swishes to the edge of the pool and lifts herself up on her elbows. It's all right to be scared. Everyone gets scared. Being scared is where brave comes from.

A big kid splashes into the pool and cold water sprays over her. She flinches and steps back. It's true, Grandma said. Being scared makes you brave.

She shakes her head and hugs her arms against her wet togs. Her poking-out belly.

You think all these kids weren't scared the first time they got in the big pool? They all stood and shivered like you and wondered how deep the water was. I will hold on to you. The whole time. I won't let you go.

She takes a step. The puddle of water on the concrete wraps

around her feet. Grandma nods at her and holds out her arms. That's a girl.

The scared feeling in her tummy—a bit excited too. She wants to feel the water around her shoulders. To kick her feet and not hit the bottom. To swim.

She takes a deep breath. She decides to be brave. She steps on to the edge. Grandma smiles and flicks her palms across the water. Bree-Anna squats. Breaks the surface of the water with her own fingers. Swims her fingers through it. It resists. She drops onto one thigh and swings her legs over the edge. Sits on the edge. Her legs dangle in the water. She can't see the bottom.

Grandma wraps her hands around her hips.

Bree-Anna shivers.

How do you feel?

Bree-Anna nods her head.

Brave? Grandma says.

Bree-Anna nods.

Grandma's hands tight, bracing her.

Slide in, she says.

Bree-Anna lets gravity take her. The water swirls around her, her feet have nothing to touch, she kicks and wriggles.

Relax, Grandma says and pulls her closer. Bree-Anna wraps her arms around her neck. The water tightens around them. Declan pops up behind Grandma's shoulder. Bobs up and down on his toes. Disappears. A fish.

There, you did it, Grandma said. Brave girl.

You're not brave. You are dumb. Fat and dumb. Did Baby say that?

Baby?

When he said you're burning up, she thought she would catch fire. She got scared.

Let me see, he said. He pulled away the sheet.

He took Baby and threw her on the floor.

He bent over her and his funny sticky-out hair smelled like dirty bathwater. Oily. Dreadlocks, he had told her last night when he came to take Mummy out. You got funny hair, she said. And he said, Dreadlocks. Touch them. And she did. Like knots, she said, and he laughed.

The smell of them now made her sick. She squirmed and pushed away from him.

I have to see if you have a rash, he said.

He unbuttoned her pyjamas. The skin on his fingers scratched her chest and her tummy. Over and over while he looked for the rash.

A rash will kill you, he said, and leaned into her and pinched her and squeezed and twisted her skin. She squealed. But not very loud because she was sick and hot and she felt floppy and tired.

He pulled at the elastic on her pyjama pants. Lifted her backside and dug his nails into her bum cheeks and pulled down her pants.

What are you doing? Declan stood at the door.

He hoisted up her pants and turned to him. Go and tell your mother your sister is sick.

Declan stood there. Not moving.

Go on, hurry up, the troll said.

Declan spun around and down the hall. The troll pulled the sheet up to her chin and put his lips almost in her ear. You say a word and I'll kill ya. You hear? She nodded. Sweat moist on her temples.

He stood up and then Mummy was there, in the door, wrapping her dressing gown around her. The troll walked up to her and put his hand in her gown. Touched her boob. But he didn't pinch it like he pinched hers. Mummy laughed at him and swatted his hand away. Go away, she said. Make me a coffee.

She turned to her side and threw up all over the bed. Mummy was mad as hell.

You say a word and I'll kill ya. You hear? She's forgotten he said that. She made herself forget. And he didn't come back. The mans don't always come back after a sleepover. So, she let herself forget. Made herself forget.

Then he came back. He was a mountain in her mummy's bed and he smiled at her. Mummy was still asleep. She pretended to Baby she was thinking about the party. About chips and lollies and games and pass-the-parcel.

The way I see it we got two options. I kill ya or you die.

Baby? Is being dead better?

How come she has two monsters to think about?

You die of thirst first.

Baby, what do I do?

Baby?

Baby isn't going to answer. Baby is just a doll. A dumb doll. Plastic, not real.

A kick in the sole of her foot. Spasms shoot up her spine.

'You dead yet?' he asks.

CHRISTMAS EVE

Jake keys his PIN into the machine. The machine flashes '*transaction approved*', and he lets out a breath. It could have gone either way. He tucks the brown paper bag under his arm. The chick behind the counter, Eloise—he remembers her name—smiles at him and says, 'Merry Christmas,' with what seems like genuine Christmas cheer.

'You too,' Jake says, but her words scrape at the hollow pit inside him.

He stashes the bottle of rum safely on the passenger seat of his car. He takes a spearmint leaf lolly from the white paper bag on the dash. There's only three left. He crumples the bag closed and puts it in his pocket.

There seems to be more cops than usual around town. Because of Christmas maybe, or something else going on. Maybe because of him. He knows that's not likely, but he does what he has been doing all week and takes the long way around. He avoids the highway, crosses it instead, passes the supermarket, the ugly old brown house with the rampant bougainvillea, and takes a right, up the hill, to Hill Rise Road.

The front door of number thirty-eight smiles wide open.

Two cars are parked in the driveway and another couple line the kerb. A Christmas Eve do at the house, he guesses. He slows, but he dare not stop, remembering the man writing down his number plate. He weaves through the curly roads to the top of the estate, across the top of the hill where the bush still tangles off to the west. He takes a right at the old cemetery and he ends up out of town. A few k's later, he takes a skinny road sloping down the river. He'd thought, once upon a time, when he lived in fairy-tale land, that he could bring La-Li here, to fish, maybe to swim when she was older. Carla, predictably, considered the idea dangerous, as though he had proposed dangling her from a ten-storey building by her ankles.

The bollards designed to keep vehicles off the river bank were washed away in the floods, so Jake has been able to take his car as far as he dares into the scrubby regrowth.

Here is his current home.

The fire coals are still warm and it takes little effort to get them smouldering again. Jake's life has hit a new low. He doesn't think it has ever been lower. Never has he lived in his car before. But the essence of him, the bit of him that is a perfectionist, that wouldn't allow grass to get patchy and weedy, or a gate to hang off its hinges, still rules his actions. He's cobbled together a lean-to, segregated an area for toileting. Smoke and mirrors, if he is honest with himself. While he can believe he is doing all right living on a riverbank, he can avoid going back to the power station and facing his now ex-boss, getting his stuff from his quarters. The longer he can stick it out here, the longer before he has to face what he did last time he saw La-Li.

But tomorrow is Christmas Day. He promised he would see her on Christmas Day and he, as far as he can remember, has never broken a promise to her.

Jake rummages through the esky in the car boot and makes

a ham and tomato sandwich. He sits on a tree stump and watches the smoke loiter in the still air before it disperses toward the river. The brown river rushes by as though it has somewhere to go. The sandwich plunges his gut back into the nausea that has plagued him for days. He forces himself to bite it, the mushy softness squeezes the nausea tighter. He gags and swallows. The rest of the sandwich he tosses into the bushes.

He gulps down some water, but it is the rum that is niggling at the back of his mind. Calling him, luring him like a wanton woman. Jake smiles to himself. Would he swap the rum for a wanton woman, any woman, Carla?

He's a social drinker. That's what he argued when Carla told him he drank too much. There is nothing social about sitting on his lonesome, on a riverbank, demolishing a bottle of rum on Christmas Eve. He knows it. He knew it when he bought it. When he thought he was heading back to camp, but at the last moment turned into the pub, wondering if he even had enough money for a bottle of rum.

His brothers' father was a drinker. For the short time he was in Jake's life, their home smelled of fermenting sweat. One morning, his mother prepared his school lunch and served him breakfast around the prostrate body of the unconscious man he was told to call dad. The kitchen stunk of vomit but his mother scowled to herself and pretended like it was any other morning. She kicked 'dad' out not long after that. Jake decided on that morning he would never be 'a drunk'.

Definitions, however, can be slippery.

The humidity weighs on him like a wet blanket. A storm cloud bears down from the west. He'll be sheltering in the car again tonight. The car gets mustier and more sickening by the day.

The rum smells molasses sweet when he cracks the lid.

With warm Coke and some of his precious ice, a layer forms over his sickness. A coat for the guilt.

What if he turned up at Carla's tomorrow? Sandy wouldn't let him in the house. Not in a pink fit. And if she did, there would be La-Li in front of the Christmas tree with a jungle of wrapping paper and gifts. *What have you bought me, Daddy?* She wouldn't say that. Carla has taught her better manners, but she would think it. All kids think it. *What have you bought me, Daddy?* Nothing. I spent the last of my money on a bottle of rum.

Too bad he opened it already. They might have taken it back. He swallows another mouthful, the Coke still warm, bubbling on his tongue.

He can't even ring her. His phone's flat as a tack and he's got nothing to charge it with. His charger is still at the power station. In his quarters, with every other thing he owns. Instead of sitting on the river like a homeless fuck, he should have gone and got his stuff.

He should have kept his temper instead of throwing a table. La-Li's sob reverberates through his ears again and he pushes the pain away with a good few mouthfuls of rum. Cicadas' shrill shrieks deafen him.

Life is full of shoulds. He should have done whatever he could to stop Carla leaving. He should have done an apprenticeship when he had the chance. He should have listened to Carla when she said Stinky Gully sucked. He should have been better. A better father, a better husband, a better lover, a better provider. Better.

His breathing quickens and he recognises the tears will come soon. He wipes his face, almost punches himself with the determination not to cry. What would it be like to never see La-Li again? For her to grow and change and for her to forget him. He imagines walking down the street and seeing her and she glances at him and keeps walking because she doesn't know who he is. That could happen. A sob escapes and he gives in, he sobs, he sobs loud and hard, his face buried in his hands, his fingers clawing his head. Snot streams from his nose. His nails pierce his skin. *Idiot, idiot, idiot.*

He picks up the bottle of rum and heaves it at the fire. It smashes and sizzles on the coals.

He tastes the salt of snot in his mouth, sticking like glue on his upper lip. He wipes it away with his sleeve. He lifts his head to the sky, his teeth clenched.

The black storm cloud thrusts its knuckle into the blue sky. It boils, agitated swirling, determined to upset the peace.

There was another baby. A baby he didn't fight hard enough for. If he doesn't fight for La-Li, he might as well be dead.

He can't stay here.

He douses the fire, packs up his gear. His body smells of dirty river baths. If he is going to see La-Li, if he is going to get on his hands and knees and beg for forgiveness, he needs at least to be clean.

He knows where he has to go. The other place he has been avoiding.

The other person he has been avoiding.

That Jake guy turns up at the bottle-o during Eloise's shift. He slouches around touching bottles, his shoulders hunched. He smells like something died and he needs a shave. A rough and ready handsome guy, regardless. Would he let her photograph him? He probably doesn't even remember her name. He chooses the cheapest bottle of rum on the shelf and places it on the counter, barely able to look up at her. What would she say? *I'm a photographer and I want take your photograph.* It sounds like a pickup line. *Come up and see my etchings. Be my muse.* She imagines the actual event. His place, her place, some other place, the discomfort of getting out the camera, being behind it. His squirming in front of it. How do people do it? How do they get those shots of people looking so unselfconscious? Full of character and personality. Their lives reflected in their eyes. She is never going to get something for the portfolio. Hopeless. He keys in his PIN, stares at the machine and seems relieved when it's approved. She rips off the paper receipt and hands it to him with the cheeriest 'Merry Christmas' she can manage.

He smiles back, but there's no Merry in it. There wasn't much Merry in her farewell either. Fake it till you make it. She yawns, so tired she feels hungover.

The shop empties for the briefest moment. Christmas Eve is the busiest day—got to get loaded up for Christmas. Family and booze, that's what it is all about. Most people go to the big cheap discount places in town; it's hard to compete. But if they forgot something, or they don't mind the bigger mark-up, they'll come in. Often for last-minute gifts. Maybe she should get a nice bottle of whiskey for her dad. He is always the hardest to buy for, especially now. He doesn't drink much anymore, not that he ever did, maybe he shouldn't at all, these days. Who knows what it would do to him? Put him to sleep might be a good scenario. She peruses the whiskey shelf. Remembers the cost of the plane ticket to be paid off. Even with her staff discount, she couldn't justify even the middle of the range bottle. Christmas Eve must be the most expensive day of the goddamn year to fly anywhere.

She checks her phone. Still no reply from Mike. She shoves it back in her pocket.

A middle-aged man saunters in, followed by a yummy mummy looking rushed and harried. The quiet was too good to last. She yawns, a gigantic yawn, and her head splits with a sudden sharp headache. She winces.

The middle-aged man stares up at the reds. The yummy mummy has her eyes all over the Baileys and expensive spirits. One of the likely lads slinks in the door and heads to the beer fridge.

Eloise picks up the phone and dials internal. 'Maggie, when you get a chance, can you make me a latte? Real strong, real big.'

'Recovering from a big night out?' Maggie sounds like she's sharing her attention with her bar work.

'I spent the night with Amber.'

'Oh.' Maggie sounds taken back. 'They heard something?'

The middle-aged man dumps three bottles of expensive red on the counter.

'Sorry, I've got a customer.' She hangs up.

A constant stream of customers full of Christmas cheer keeps her awake, though bleary. Her head pounds. She finds a couple of Panadol in her bag. They take the sharp edge off, but she still feels like her head is in a bucket of sharp ice. She doesn't have time to check her messages, but she wishes that coffee would come.

A pair of girls dump a six-pack of UDLs on the bench.

'You got ID?' Eloise asks.

'I left it at home,' the chick says, her midriff bared, belly button pierced. 'I'm eighteen, honest.'

The other girl slides in behind her friend, trying to disappear.

'No ID, no service.'

'Aww, come on, it's Christmas.' The girl sprawls on the counter, smiling.

Eloise picks up the cans and puts them under the counter.

'I'll put it aside for you, and you can go and get your ID,' she says.

'Bitch,' the girl spits and stomps off, knocking a cardboard display for cheap sparkling over.

Maggie comes in through the back door with a coffee.

'Thank god.' She takes the coffee.

'You look like shit.' Maggie goes around the counter and rights the display.

'Amber didn't sleep, so I couldn't sleep.' Eloise breathes in the smooth coffee aroma and takes a sip.

'Oh?'

'I've been dropping in and out, visiting. Amber's not easy to spend time with at the best of times. I just... anyhow, I stayed there. Hold on.' Eloise rings up a carton of beer for a guy, grins Merry Christmas cheer at him.

'God, I need a break,' she says and sips at her coffee.

'Yeah, busy inside too. Charlie just got in, but I think I'll have to stay back late.'

'I gotta leave early—I've got to go to the airport.'

'Oh? You going somewhere?' Maggie grins, knowing this is as likely as Santa granting all their wishes in the morning.

'I wish,' Eloise says. She turns the coffee around in her hand.

'So, Amber?'

'She is beside herself. I worry about her boy too. I don't know what to do. She can't still be alive. What happens when they find her body? What happens if they never find her body?'

'Why would Amber let the girl walk off down the highway on her own?'

Eloise shrugs.

'Nothing from the police?'

'Not according to Amber. Are they competent at all?'

Eloise shakes her head. 'Amber sat there all night, staring at the landline. She thinks Bree-Anna will call her on it. I tried to make her go to bed…' She shrugs. 'I don't think she's slept since Sunday.'

'Would you?'

'Probably not.'

A couple comes to the counter.

'I better go,' says Maggie. 'Let me know if they hear anything else.'

'Sure,' says Eloise. 'Has Mike called today?'

'Yeah, earlier. I didn't speak to him though.'

'Okay.' Eloise smiles at the couple. 'Got a big day planned for tomorrow?' she says to the couple, not really caring at all. Caring about as much as she'd care for a rat having eaten Ratsak.

She can't put it off any longer and in the next lull in customer action, she dials Mike.

'Hello,' he answers, businesslike.

'It's me,' she says.

'I know,' he says.

'Is she…'

'Yes,' he replies.

'Okay.' She blows out a breath. 'Did you get my texts?'

'Which one?'

'I need to finish early today. I can't find anyone to cover for me.'

'It's got to be the busiest day of the year. Can't it wait? Is it your father?'

'No,' she says. 'It's…'

'Just a moment,' he interrupts. 'I'll see if the paper work is in my office.'

Eloise hears shuffling and white noise, a child calls 'Daddy' and Daddy—Mike—calls back, 'In a minute honey,' then a door closing and Mike's heavy breath in the phone. 'I might be able to get away later. We could meet up. Usual place. Around six?'

Eloise groans. 'I can't. I wish I could, but today is a mess.'

'How's the pub?'

'Busy, I got the bottle-o shift.' A woman arrives at the counter with cheap Chardonnay. Eloise smiles at her. 'Just a moment.'

'You'll be done by six then?' Mike says.

'Yeah, but I got to get away early, around three-thirty or four. I have to go to the airport.'

'The airport?'

'Yeah.' Eloise takes a deep breath. The woman scowls at her. Eloise covers the receiver. 'The boss,' she mouths. The woman taps her credit card on the counter. Eloise shakes her head and turns her back.

'I'm picking up Anthony,' she whispers.

'Anthony!'

'Yeah, I paid for him to fly up.'

'Oh, Eloise, you idiot. You think your mum needs that added stress now?'

'Excuse me,' the woman says behind her back.

Eloise turns. Two other customers have formed a line behind her. 'Just a minute,' she says and turns back to the phone.

'I'm leaving early,' she says clearly. 'I'll get someone from the bar to cover. It will only be an hour or so until Karen starts her shift.'

'You know he will never change. He's a no-hope junkie. Don't come to me when it all goes pear-shaped.'

'What would be the point? You're never there!'

'I just offered to see you today. Don't put that on me. I got responsibilities coming out of my ears. I don't need you...'

'Oh, Mike.' Eloise's nose scrunches up, bitterness and

sarcasm oozing into her voice. 'I wouldn't want to be a nuisance.'

'And yet… here you are,' he hisses back.

'Go fuck yourself.' Eloise steps further away from the counter. 'In fact, go fuck your wife.'

She hangs up the phone and turns to face her customers, who stare, stunned, back at her.

Very bad career move.

The petrol light comes on a bit over halfway to his mother's house. He glances at the light, every second praying, though he is far from a praying man, that he doesn't run out. More than anything, he doesn't think he can handle the embarrassment of allowing himself to run out of petrol.

He shifts in the car seat and swears to himself. *You're a dickhead, a complete dickhead.* He leaves the motorway at the shopping centre, the car park packed with last-minute Christmas shoppers. Big boxes and bikes being stowed in car boots. What did La-Li want for Christmas? What would he buy her if he could buy her anything? She didn't want for much. A scooter would be cool. She could scoot along the boardwalk. He could follow, watching her hair flying behind her, her little legs scooping through the air. Carla would probably make her wear a helmet. Maybe a helmet was a good idea.

The car lurches and he thinks, *this is it*, and waits for it to splutter to a stop, but the car keeps travelling. When he finally reaches his mother's street and her two-storey pale-brick house, his limbs go heavy and he struggles to initiate the movement of getting out of the car.

Jake opens the front door without knocking. Silence in the house. His stomach churns. It's been like a washing machine since he left Carla's house. Now it is on spin cycle, turning bile and shit and alcohol. He walks slowly to the back of the house and the kitchen and finds it empty.

'Mum?' he calls. He knocks on her bedroom door and no one answers.

He turns and bumps into his brother. 'Shit, you scared me. Don't sneak up on people like that!'

'Whatever.' His brother shrugs and heads off in the opposite direction.

'Hey, where's Mum?'

'Shopping,' his brother says over his shoulder.

He wanders back into his bedroom and Jake follows. The dark room smells fruity, like rotten socks and stale air. Should he tell him to clean his room?

His brother flops on his bed and picks up the game controls and puts the headphones on his head. 'The cops been looking for you,' he says.

'What?' Jake leans on the cluttered dresser.

His brother presses some buttons and the game perks back to life. 'The cops have been round here looking for you. Early in the week. Monday, I think. Mum's got a number to call.'

Jake's stomach drops like a boulder in his gut. Carla made a complaint about him. Or Sandy. Bitch, bitch, bitch. Now he will never get to see La-Li.

'Any grog in the house?'

His brother looks at him with hooded eyes as if to say, *really*? 'Mum's got wine in the fridge. Don't drink it all.'

Jake's lip twitches. 'You should clean your room. It fuckin' stinks, you pig.'

The Riesling in a box tastes like he imagines sweet petrol would taste. Nevertheless, he manages to get through two glasses before his mother arrives with the rustling of shopping bags.

She dumps the bags on the table. 'Jake, you look like something the cat dragged in,' she says, her voice flat before she calls more loudly, 'Patrick, get the groceries out of the boot.'

'In a minute,' Jake's brother calls back.

'Now!' his mother shouts, like she did when Jake was a kid and it always made him jump. His stomach lurches, startled, even though it is not him she shouts at. 'What's going on, Jake?' She pushes her glasses back on her face and fixes a look at him.

'Carla's a bitch,' he says.

'I know that already, what's going on with you? I had the cops around here Monday. I've been trying to call you. And I texted you. Several times.'

'Like I said, Carla's a bitch.'

'No, it wasn't about Carla. It was something to do with that little girl.'

'Yeah, La-Li.' Heat rises in Jake's body as it remembers the shame. He drains the last of the Riesling in his glass. He reaches for the box.

'Don't drink all my wine,' his mother says over her shoulder while she searches through a pile of papers and bills on top of the microwave.

'I'll buy you another one.' And he knows immediately he can't. 'When I have some money,' he says more quietly.

She turns suddenly. 'You lost your job again?'

'I'll get another one. I always do.' He wipes imaginary crumbs from the clean tabletop.

'Well, I will want wine for tomorrow. Will you have a job by then?' She stands with her hand on her hip, her eyes wide, and Jake feels ten years old again.

'No,' he says and pushes the box away, his glass still empty.

'Are you staying for Christmas?'

Jake nods.

She turns around and goes back to her searching. 'What about Alannah? Are you bringing her over?'

'I don't know.'

'Have you asked Carla?' She gives up on the pile of papers. 'Maybe I put it in my handbag.' Everything starts coming out of her tattered handbag. Tissues, wallet, old shopping lists, envelopes. 'Shit, I meant to post that,' she says, putting the envelope in the middle of the table.

His brother dumps bags of groceries on the table. 'Why can't Jake help?' he says, and inspects where the plastic bags have cut into his fingers.

'We're talking. Did you hang that washing out?' his mother replies.

'Yeess,' Patrick says and disappears back down the hall.

His mother gives up on the handbag and opens up a grocery bag. 'Give me a hand with this frozen stuff.'

Jake takes the bag and unpacks frozen peas and corn and ice-cream into the freezer. His mother bangs about in cupboards with cans of baked beans and spaghetti and tomatoes.

'I got a nice ham for tomorrow. Smoked. I got some lollies and things that Alannah will like too. I wasn't sure if she was coming. Marie and Peter are coming over in the afternoon for a wine.'

'Who are they?'

'The neighbours. Remember, he had a heart attack last year. She works at the bakery. I got some nice cheese and crackers to have when they are here.' She starts handing him cold cheese and butter for the fridge.

'I don't think people with bad hearts are supposed to eat cheese.'

'It's Christmas! That's why I want to see my grandchild.'

'I don't know if La-Li can come.'

'Why? You have a right to see your daughter on Christmas Day. She has a right to see you. I keep telling you, you got to talk to a lawyer, get a proper agreement drawn up. What did you buy her for Christmas?'

'I don't have any money,' Jake says.

His mother pauses, sighs, and takes bags of chips and nuts out of a bag and walks back toward the pantry. 'What's Carla got the shits about now?'

Jake shrugs and takes a sponge cake from the bag. He can't admit to his mother that it is his fault. That he doesn't deserve to see her. That La-Li is probably too scared to be in the same room as him. That he is a violent tyrant. 'What do you want me to do with this?' He holds up the sponge.

'Leave it there, I'm going to make a trifle this afternoon. Alannah liked my trifle last year. Remember?'

He doesn't remember.

His brother struggles in with more bags. 'Is that the last of it?' his mother asks.

'Yes,' Patrick says. 'Did you get my pies?'

'I got your pies.'

Patrick starts unpacking the bags and handing things to Jake or his mother, depending on what it is. 'You tell him about the cops coming on Monday?'

'Yeah, you know what I did with that card? With the phone number on it?' His mother inspects the label on a box of jelly.

'You put it by the computer,' Patrick says, handing Jake a packet of frozen pies for the freezer.

'Of course!' She disappears out of the room, wiping her hands over her hips as though they are wet but they are not.

Jake takes the card from her and barely looks at it before putting it in his pocket.

'Don't you care?' his brother says.

'What the fuck is it to you?' Jake answers.

'Jake! Language.' His mother points her finger at him

'Some kid is missing and he doesn't even care.' His brother peers at him.

Missing.

Jake takes the card from his pocket and stares at the name on the card.

'Who's missing?' His heart skips and leaps. La-Li. Though he knows it is not her.

'That little girl from Stinky Gully. On Sunday morning. On the highway. God knows what her mother was thinking, letting her walk down there on her own.' His mother tips the red jelly crystals into a bowl.

Jake sinks into the kitchen chair. The fat girl in the pink T-shirt.

'They reckon your car is on some CCTV. They want to know if you saw anything,' his brother says.

'Did you see her?' his mother asks.

Jake rubs his cheeks, the bristles of his unshaven skin crackle under his hands. 'Yeah, I saw her. Shit. They found her?'

'I wouldn't be giving you the card if they found her, Jake,' his mother says, handing him the phone.

The traffic on the highway is manic. She shut up shop and put a sign in the window: back in an hour. It will shit people off, but she convinces herself she doesn't care. Customers will come back later or they won't. It's not like it will send Mike broke. And if it does, serve him right the sanctimonious using bastard. She is done with him and his crappy job in the crappy pub with no atmosphere and food fit for prison. Mike is scum of the earth and she is better off without him. She won't be around next year, anyway. All going well.

The airport shuffles with people dragging bags, hugging and kissing long lost loved ones, a craze of joy and Christmas carols and Eloise wants to puke, it is so sappy.

The screen announces the flight arrival and butterflies bounce about in her belly. She watches the gate, the businessmen, and the old grannies and grandpas greeting grandchildren, the families with mothers looking trashed, tugging toddlers. Did he miss the plane? Would that be a relief or disappointing? Both. He comes through the gate last, skinny as a twig. He grins at her and reveals a missing tooth. He drops his bag on the floor and grips her in a tight hug. When at last he lets her go, she searches for evidence. Glances at his arms. His eyes.

'I'm clean,' he says, noticing her looks.

'You'd better be.' She picks up his bag off the floor, but he takes it from her and drapes it over his shoulder. A bunch of kids crash past, laughing. *This is not a playground*, Eloise thinks. 'Let's get out of this shit hole.'

'You still driving this old bomb?' Anthony jokes when she clicks open the boot.

'What else am I going to do?' she says, her guard still up. She wants to let it down, but he has to prove himself first. She is not sure how.

'How's Dad?' he asks when they are out of the car park.

'Depends on the day,' Eloise says.

'He was all right with me coming home? I mean, he didn't do his nut or anything?'

'He doesn't know. Neither of them knows.'

'Great,' Anthony replies, 'so I am the Christmas surprise. That should disappoint everyone.'

Eloise glances at him but can't tell if he is joking or not.

'Will he remember who I am even?'

'He's not got that bad,' Eloise says. 'Maybe he could be better if we could get him to the doctor.' *Please help*, she pleads silently.

He asks where she is going next year, what she meant on the phone, and she tells him she is getting a portfolio together for a Bachelor of Fine Arts. She's probably not good enough to get in. She already got an extension. Cause of when Dad went missing. She's already in their bad books. They'll be looking for a reason to reject her.

'Yeah well, you should have done that from the beginning. Instead of going down the law track. Whatever made you think you would make a good lawyer?'

Eloise grunts a laugh. 'You know Dad. He wasn't going to let me do anything arty farty.'

'And now?'

'I haven't told him yet.'

'He'll hit the roof.'

'Yeah, well. He might not remember.'

'Then he'll hit the roof every time you remind him. Like it is new news every time. A constant explosion. I like this song,' he says, turning up the radio. He taps his fingers on his knees and sings along and if anything was to convince her he was clean it was this, knowing a new song on the radio, words and all.

'I'm going to go back,' he says. 'To finish my sound engineering. There's a good college in Brisbane now. I don't have to go back to Sydney.'

She doesn't say anything; she hopes, but she is scared to hope.

'So,' he says, 'Stinky Gully has been in the news.'

Eloise remembers the posters on the back seat. She should have thought to take them into the airport with her. Ask someone to put them up. She's been sharing the missing posts on Facebook. That's more effective, isn't it?

'Yeah, it's Amber's kid.'

'I figured that. How's the whore taking it?'

She gives him a dirty look. 'Don't call her a whore.'

'Like you don't think she's a whore. So, who do you think did it?'

'How would I know?'

'I don't know. You know everyone in town, don't you?'

Eloise shrugs. 'It was probably an out of towner. Some sicko insomniac passing through. Saw his chance and took it.'

'Poor kid. Do you think she's dead already?'

'I don't know. It seems likely. Amber thinks she's going to ring on her landline because her teacher said she made all the kids memorise their phone numbers.'

'Sounds like she's grasping at straws.'

'I don't know how it can end well.' She imagines Amber alone all day, fixated on the phone. Did she think to eat, to feed Declan? Did she do as she was told and call her mother?

'You've spoken to her today?'

Guilt gnaws at her. 'I spent the whole night with her last night. She promised me she'd call her mum when I left this morning. She's got her mum now.'

'What do you mean?'

'They had some sort of falling out. They haven't spoken for aeons.'

She looks over at him; he's watching the city pass by through the window. His cheekbones protrude from his face. 'Mum's going to want to feed you up,' she says.

'Things have changed around here,' he says.

She shrugs. 'There are some new buildings. This road is new.'

'I bet Stinky Gully is the same.'

'Huh,' she says. 'Even Stinky Gully is not immune from progress. The Randalls sold off their farm and now it grows houses like weeds. They all look the same. Full of renters. The town is not the same country town it used to be. The school's growing, new buildings all over the place. You won't recognise it.'

The road hums beneath them, the sun flashes through the window. Towering over the high-rises is the creep of a storm cloud, purple like a bruise. The traffic slows to a standstill.

'Christmas Eve,' Eloise complains.

'She might not be dead,' Anthony says. 'Sometimes weirdos kidnap the kids. Keep them. Bring them up as their own.'

'You think?' Eloise says, changing to the right lane, which creeps marginally faster.

'I don't know. It could have been opportunistic. Someone who knew the kid. Someone the kid knew.'

'Like it could be someone local?'

'Maybe,' Anthony says. 'They always say it's the quiet ones that live at home with their mothers. They should check all them out. Put them on a register.'

'Yeah right,' Eloise says, 'I can see that getting past the bleeding hearts. Damn it, I hope we get home before this storm hits.'

Anthony winds the window down. 'Tropical air.' He sniffs. 'Smells like home.' He turns back to her. 'How's the pub? Still working there? Will I recognise it?'

Eloise laughs. 'Well, considering I shut up the bottle-o early to come get you and told the boss to go fuck himself, that is an open question.'

'What, old Kevie? What did he do?'

'No, some other guy owns it now. He's got a few pubs. Thinks Stinky Gully is up-and-coming and worth investment. He's a stuck-up wanker with a prissy wife.'

'Sounds like you got the hots for him.'

'Not likely,' she says.

'Pity,' he says. 'I was hoping you'd put a word in for me. I'll be wanting some work. Maybe I can do some cleaning. You got some clients, some real pigs you want to palm off on me. I'm accustomed to pig-sties.'

'How about Colin Randall?' She laughs.

'Colin effing Randall. I'd forgotten all about that dweeb. He should be on that register. Someone should check out his place for the kid.'

'I was there yesterday,' Eloise says.

The flash of pink in the clothes basket springs into her mind like a photograph. His more than usual weirdness. How he wouldn't let her in his mother's room. The rat noises.

She looks at her brother. 'Do you really think?'

Anthony shrugs. 'The olds are going to be all right, aren't they? About me coming? I wish you told them.'

'They'll be fine.' Eloise shifts to a higher gear. Distant lightning fires through the clouds. Her stomach churns. Colin Randall? Could it be?

They tell Jake to come straight down to the station. Not the local one, the one in the city. He has to borrow money from his mother for petrol and parking. In the foyer, he remembers how bad he smells, of river water and probably Riesling and rum too. His clothes hang on his body, damp with sweat. He presses on his hair, trying to ram it into a tidy state.

He thinks he will have to wait, but when he tells them who he is and why he is there, they take him straight into an interview room. The cop stands just inside the door while Jake pulls out a seat, the scrape echoing around the tiny white walled room.

'The Detective Inspector won't be long, sir.'

'Right,' says Jake, thinking the cop looks about twelve and when did cops get so young. The gun in his holster could only be a plaything.

'Nice to be in the air-conditioning,' Jake says.

The cop nods a curt nod and cuts conversation by staring intently at the ceiling.

The Detective Inspector, jaw like a Besser brick, strides in with a folder and papers. He introduces himself and the other officer without offering his hand to shake. He sits, and even sitting he looms. 'Jake Reid?'

Jake wipes his sweating hands on his pants and nods.

'Pardon?'

'Yes, sir,' Jake says.

'Of 24 Bang Drive, Coal Bank Plains? We are going to take a statement.' He waves a finger at the officer as though he is a dog being told to sit. The officer scurries to his seat, fingers poised over the keyboard, ready to type.

The cop repeats Jake's name and address.

'That's where my mum lives.'

'That's the address your car is registered at.'

'I've been out west. Working. Moving about.'

The Detective Inspector frowns, his eyebrows almost meeting in a wolf-like mono-brow. 'What about last Sunday, Mr Reid? Were you *out west*?'

'I went to visit my daughter.'

'Ah ha.' He lifts his pen above the paper. 'Tell us about last Sunday. You spent the day with your daughter?' The detective taps the end of his pen on the table and leans back.

'Yes, Alannah-Lily.'

'How old is she?'

'Five.' Jake cracks his knuckles, nervous.

'Someone can verify this?' The cop's square jaw juts into the space between them.

'My wife,' Jake squeezes out.

'Your wife?'

'My ex-wife.' He shifts in his seat. 'I thought this was about the little girl in Stinky Gully?'

'Yes, the little girl in Stinky Gully.' The Detective Inspector grins as though sharing a secret with Jake and the penny drops like an atom bomb.

'Shit!' Jake sits up straighter. 'I didn't do anything to that little girl. I wouldn't. I just... wouldn't. I just saw her.'

'On Sunday?'

'I got petrol. At Stinky Gully. I saw her walk past...' Jake's brain fuddles and he loses his words. They think he...

'She walked past?' the detective prompts.

'By the petrol station. She had like a... doll in a stroller. I thought... I thought it was a bit strange. I thought someone else was following her. Up the path. Then I went in and paid for my petrol.'

'What time was this?'

'I don't know... About eleven? Eleven-thirty?'

'You paid for the petrol?'

'I said to the guy in the petrol station, Did you see that little girl? I thought it was strange. That she was out there. On her own.'

'And this guy... the cashier at the fuel station?'

'He said he didn't see her.'

'And that's it? You got in your car and drove away? To see your daughter?'

Jake's heart bangs and trips. 'No.' He thinks he might cry. 'I saw her get into a car. As I was driving away.'

'And you can describe this car?'

'It was green. A station wagon. An awful green. Like a lime green. I never saw a car that colour before. I remember thinking, who would own a car that colour?'

'A station wagon? Make?' The Detective Inspector looks at the baby cop as if he wouldn't know this is the important bit. The bit to really write down.

'Ford Fairmont. Early eighties XD.'

'That's very specific, Mr Reid.'

'I know cars,' Jake says.

'And you didn't think to tell someone you saw this girl getting into this'—he pretends to look at his notes, though he hadn't taken any—'lime-green XD Ford Fairmont?'

'She... she...' Jake presses his fingers into his temples.

'She?'

'She looked like she was getting in willingly. She wasn't being forced. I thought someone was just picking her up.' His hands drop to the table in front of him, limp.

'Tell me about Monday, Mr Reid.'

'Monday?' Jake shakes his head.

'Where were you Monday?'

'I was... I went to see my daughter.'

'In Stinky Gully?' The Detective Inspector pulls himself forward, owning the table.

Jake backs away without thinking. 'She doesn't live in Stinky Gully anymore.'

'So, you weren't in Stinky Gully Monday?'

'I was.' He shakes his head. 'For a little while. In the morning.'

'Where exactly?'

'Around... Hill Rise Road.'

'You visiting someone there?'

'Yes.'

'At five-thirty in the morning?'

Jake sighs, his breath ragged. 'No.'

'Then what?'

'I slept in my car. I had... I had nowhere...'

The Detective Inspector starts slipping his notes into the folder. 'You got all that?' he asks the other cop.

'Yes, sir,' the baby officer replies.

'Well, we'll get this ready for you to sign,' he says, turning his grey eyebrows back to Jake and standing. 'And we'll need your wife's... your *ex-wife's* contact details.'

'I'm not lying.' Jake looks up at the tall man, his neck bent.

The Detective Inspector shakes his head and leans on the desk. His mint breath burns into Jake's face. 'You know, if we had this information earlier...' He doesn't finish the sentence. There is no need.

Lightning stabs the ground with fiery white forks. Anthony watches Stinky Gully pass by in silence. Families mill around the park for twilight Christmas carols and greasy sausages in bread cooked up by the Lions Club. They will be running for cover soon enough. Some things don't change. Eloise pulls up at their house, the house where they toddled, did homework, snuck out of windows as teenagers. The home that birthed adult dreams that have never come to pass.

They both sit unmoving. Eloise rattles the keys in her hand.

Anthony takes a deep breath and blows it out. 'Well, here goes nothing,' he says, pushing the car door open. He looks back at her. 'You coming?'

'Like a lamb to the slaughter,' she says and they grin at each other.

Eloise calls to her mother as she opens the front door. 'I got a surprise.'

Anthony hovers half in the door, half out, his bag like a shield, dangling at his knees.

Their mother steps into the foyer and stops dead. Her hand lifts and quivers in front of her mouth. 'Anthony.' The name shakes from her. As she steps toward her son, Anthony drops his bag, steps over it, and buries her in his embrace. They rock together, could have stayed that way indefinitely, except their father steps into the room.

Their mother pulls away; she can't straighten the smile on her face. 'Look who it is.' She presents Anthony to his father. *Yes, just like a lamb to the slaughter*, Eloise thinks. The two men eye each other off.

'Dad,' Anthony says and takes a step into the breach, the no man's land of floor stretching between them.

Their father takes a step back, bracing his hands on either side of the doorway. To hold himself upright? To keep himself from springing away?

'It's Anthony.' Their mother takes Anthony's elbow and gently propels him further into the house.

'I *know* who it is,' their father says. 'I'm not completely senile. Not yet. What's he doing here?'

'Come for Christmas, Daddy,' Eloise says.

'Huh, well, hide the silver,' he replies, then puts his glasses back on his face, turns and walks back to the lounge.

'He'll come around,' their mother says. 'Come into the kitchen.'

'You should have warned him.' Anthony pushes past Eloise and back out the door.

'Come back!' Their mother totters after him. 'Don't go anywhere.'

Eloise watches Anthony stride down the path, his long legs swift and sure as they used to be before. Before all the drama and disappointment. If he goes, will he find somewhere to score? Is this the sort of thing that would tip him over? In the past, it would have been. She has no reason to believe things have changed.

She follows her mother down the stairs, catches up with her when they catch him up at the car.

'Give me the keys,' he says to Eloise.

'Why, where are you going?' Eloise grips the keys hard as though he might play a game of snatch, as if they are children again.

'Where do you think I'm going?'

'Don't go, Anthony.' Their mother grips his sleeve and pulls his shoulder down, so he's crooked, bending halfway to her.

'I don't know where you are going. It's my car,' says Eloise.

'I gave it to you,' Anthony spits and steps up, his fist clenched, his mother still hanging off him like a lost child.

'Anthony,' she pleads, tears in her voice. 'It's Christmas.'

Thunder rumbles like a mountain of boulders bearing down on them.

He shakes her away and collapses against the car, slides down until he sits against it, looks up at the storm cloud-soaked sky. His mouth pulls into a grimace, his teeth grind against each other.

'I'm sorry,' he groans. 'It's all my fault.'

'It's not your fault.' Their mother falls in beside him, wraps her arm around his shoulder and pulls his head onto her shoulder.

'It is his fault,' Eloise says, and sits down on the grass facing them both. Anthony looks over their mother's head and grins at her. 'Chances are,' Eloise continues, 'if we go back in an hour's time, he won't even remember you were here already.'

'Eloise!' Her mother turns and scowls at her.

'Is he really that bad?' Anthony looks shocked.

'Not really,' Eloise replies, 'but in this case we can hope.'

Her mother and Anthony laugh through their tears. Eloise smiles to herself and plucks grass from the ground. Her brother's laughter, together with her mother's, is like medicine to her. A prescription that has been hard to fill.

The laughter ends and Anthony rubs his hands over his face and groans. 'What now?'

'The way I see it,' Eloise says, 'there are two choices. We go off and get wasted, or we go back inside and you... we face the music.'

Anthony's eyes grip hers and, *yes*, she communicates silently, *I know what is on your mind. I know how these things work*. 'You're not the centre of the universe,' she says. 'We've all got our own problems and you're either with us or you're not.'

He nods and his Adam's apple gulps up and down his throat.

'Don't listen to her,' their mother says, touching his face. 'You will always be welcome here. This is your home.'

Anthony pushes himself back up to stand, the car as his crutch. Their mother follows him up. 'I just want to go for a drive, clear my head,' he says.

Eloise's stomach tightens, because she wants to believe him. But his words, now, after what she just said, are like the wheedling of old. *Give me an inch*, they promise. *Give me an inch and trust me not to take the mile*. Anthony never did things by halves. If there is a mile to take, he will take it. Heavy drops of rain start to drip from the broiling clouds.

'Please,' he says, holding out his hand for the keys. 'I promise I'll be back in a bit. He'll have a chance to cool down. You can talk to him while I'm gone. Get him softened up.'

Eloise stabs the sharp key into her hand, closes her eyes, and holds her breath.

'You go with him, Eloise.' Their mother takes her hand, as if to take the keys. Eloise snatches them away and looks stonily back at Anthony. 'No,' she says. 'Get the fuck inside and face the music or fuck off out of our lives forever.'

'Eloise!' her mother exclaims, over her language or the sentiment, Eloise can't decide, but her heart pounds in her chest and Anthony's brown eyes dart left and right and won't look at her.

She rushes forward and grabs his arm, digs her nails into his bicep and tries to hurl him back toward the house, but he is like a rock, a block of concrete steadfast in the driveway.

'You promised me,' she hisses.

The screen door screeches and her father's heavy footfall sounds down the stairs. She feels Anthony stiffen in her grip. If he could magic himself through the metal casing of the car, she reckons he would. Her mother walks up the path to meet her father halfway.

He looks at the three of them and shakes his head. 'What are you doing out here? You'll get struck by lightning. Get inside, I made up some cordial. The ice is melting.'

The sky flashes white and bright. 'Cordial?' Anthony whispers.

Eloise shrugs. 'Cordial,' she says, and they follow their parents, side by side up the path.

They sit in the loungeroom and sip on cordial as thick and strong as tar. Outside, the wind lashes the house and the rain whips the windows.

Anthony claims to have enrolled in a sound engineering course in Brisbane. Their mother decrees this is wonderful and her father asks how he's going to pay for it, and he says Eloise is organising a job at the pub for him and Eloise thinks that is as likely as hell freezing over. She gets up and turns on the Christmas tree lights.

'Next thing we know, Eloise will go back and finish her law degree,' her father says.

Eloise shakes her head. 'No, I don't think so.'

'All those brains gone to waste,' he says, and she wonders how it comes about that he is picking on her at this minute when the ruination of her brother lolls in the lounge chair, such easy pickings, just half an hour ago begging for the use of a car to carry him to the nearest drug contact. Maybe. Or maybe to go and clear his head. That's all, nothing more. Pain taps at her forehead. *Tap, tap, tap*, her headache back again. The sweet stickiness of cordial sits slick in the back of her throat.

'You and Amber both,' her father continues. 'You both had brains to go do something with your lives. Of course, Amber got an excuse, not a good one. She should have kept herself for when she got married. She was still a kid when she had that kid. Is that the one that's dead?' He turns to her mother and Eloise's stomach lurches.

'No,' her mother says, patting his forearm. 'It's the younger one that's gone missing. She's not dead. Just lost.'

'Lost,' he grunts. 'Who loses children? She shouldn't have taken her eyes off her.'

'I got some stuff I got to do,' Eloise says and stands. She retreats to her room with sticky tape and Christmas wrap, dumps it on her bed, and stares at it. Her head throbs like a ball is bouncing from one temple to the other. *Bang thump crash*, a game of torturous tennis.

It is not triple zero she should ring. This is not an emergency. The local cop shop would have shut up shop at this hour. They wouldn't be dealing with this anyhow. It is too big. She bangs her phone on her forehead. There's a number on the Facebook posts. The ones she has been sharing for days.

She jumps when the phone rings. She looks at the number: the pub. Mike?

'Hello?'

'Hey, Eloise?' Maggie whispers into the phone. 'I thought I'd give you the heads-up. Mike called and Charlie told him you shut up early. He's mad as hell.'

'Whatever,' Eloise says, picking at the threads on the end of her T-shirt. 'If he gives me any trouble, I'll just have to have a word with his wife.' She knows she would never do that.

'She deserves better than him,' Maggie says. 'You talk to Amber? They heard anything? There's nothing on the news.'

'No. Hey, do you know Colin Randall?'

'No, should I?'

'Not really. I got to go.'

'Hey, by the way, who did you pick up from the airport? Anyone interesting?'

'Anthony, my brother.'

'He clean?'

'Seems to be.'

'Hopefully it will stay that way. He sticking around?'

'I don't know. Maybe.'

'I'd like to meet him. You have a good Christmas. I'll see you at work—maybe!'

'You too.'

She hangs up. Eloise grips the phone. Squeezes it as if it will spurt a decision from inside.

Damn it. What has she got to lose?

She finds the phone number on one of her posts and dials.

The woman with the telephone voice sounds incredulous when she says, 'You saw pink clothes in the dirty clothes basket? Anything else suspicious?'

She feels stupid. This is so dumb. 'It's probably nothing. It's just, he's a weird man, a bit creepy, you know. I heard a noise. It might have been rats. I thought it was rats.'

She gives up Randall's address and describes his ugly old

green car, and the official telephone voice says they'll look into it and thanks her for ringing.

Dumb idea. She's been imagining things. Making up grand stories. She hopes it doesn't come back on her. That he doesn't complain to Amber. Amber's not going to give a flying shit, she realises. She should call Amber. She knows she should. She just can't.

While Jake bunkers down in the police station, a storm passes over. The city's lights reflect red and white smudges on the wet concrete. Jake stands under a tree at the front of the station. A gust of wind flares down the footpath and the tree above him spits raindrops at him. His feet move him onto the sodden footpath.

Somewhere out there is a little girl. Buried? Covered in leaves? Dumped in a river? Is it too much to hope for that she is alive? That her blood is not on his hands?

Somewhere out there is a mother and a father with an empty space where their daughter should be. He imagines an empty space where La-Li should be. To walk into her bedroom, he imagines the bedroom at Stinky Gully. That is the one he knows. To walk into that bedroom and see her bed flat, devoid of the shape that should be there. To see her toys, her dolls, her books, still, frozen without play.

Holy fuck, what has he done?

He shivers, the wet on his shoulders smearing over the sweat of the day. He wants a jacket, a jumper; he wants arms around his shoulders, hugging him. Holding him close, comforting him. Yes, he wants Carla. He will always want Carla.

Grief drains through him, a thick sadness presses on his shoulders, and he aches. Around him office workers rush, blank faced, stony. He stops, confused. He can't remember where he left the car. He becomes debris in the river of commuters. A man, his faced glued to his mobile, bumps into him and glares at him, mumbling *fucking dickhead* as he steps around the boulder of Jake. The stuck in the mud Jake.

Cars slosh past. People slice by, their touch icy. Prickly. Jake turns in a circle, staring back at where he came. Did he even come from this way? He looks up at the building towering over him, tries to place where he is.

'You all right?' A warm hand wraps around his forearm.

A young woman has hold of him.

'I… can't…' Jake splutters.

The hand around his arm drags him across the footpath and leans him against a shop window, away from the flood of people.

'Are you sick?' The piercing in the girl's lip glints in the street light.

Jake rubs his face. 'Oh god, I'm such an idiot. I can't remember where I left my car.'

The woman smiles. 'That happened to me once.' She lets go of his arm. 'I had to retrace my steps. Where have you been? Start at the beginning.'

'The beginning.' Jake laughs. 'That's a real good question.'

The pierced girl is right; when he retraces his steps, he remembers the car park he left his car in. The traffic out of town sludges along and he rehearses the conversation he will have with Carla.

The road is dry at her house. The storm passed around here. Every rehearsed word of what he wants to say leaves him. His head empty. The yellow lights of the house glow warm against the darkened sky. The mumble of a television and the comfort of food cooking rises like a barbed-wire fence before him.

The broken gate scrapes over the concrete path. The stairs shudder beneath his step. The door opens before he can knock.

'Jake.'

A golf ball in his throat. 'Carl.'

He closes his eyes. His heart beats a million beats a second. The sob rises like a moan. He doesn't get a chance to stop it before it is out there. On the door step. A splutter of tears. He opens his eyes. She is still standing there, her arms crossed like a shield, the door frame her armour.

Sandy calls from inside, 'Carla?' and Carla pulls the door closed. She shoves Jake's shoulders, propels him down the stairs. She follows.

She gets into his car.

He climbs into the driver's seat and looks at her.

She stares out the passenger window, the light a halo around her face.

'Carla?' He reaches toward her.

'For fuck's sake, Jake.' She turns her head. 'What were you thinking, coming here?'

Jake's hands fall into his lap. 'I'm sorry. I'm an idiot.'

Sandy appears at the top of the stairs, a menacing shadow.

Carla sighs and flicks her hand toward the windscreen. 'Just drive.'

Jake turns the ignition. Sandy runs down the stairs. He pulls away from the gutter onto the street. In the rear-vision mirror, he can see Sandy on the footpath, staring after them. 'Won't she be mad?'

'She'll get over it,' Carla says, looking over her shoulder.

The road bounces beneath them, giving rhythm to their silence. Carla's perfume permeates the car like an aphrodisiac. The same scent it always was.

Jake weaves through the tidy suburbs to the river. He stops above the boardwalk under a row of weeping figs. The car shudders to stillness. The tree's leaves cavort gently with the breeze.

'You know you stink. This car stinks. Have you been living in it or something?' Carla says.

Jake grips the steering wheel. 'I'm sorry, about the table. The other day. I'll pay for it.'

'The table was a piece of shit. I hated it,' Carla says.

'Oh fuck. La-Li, did I scare her?' Jake's head slumps against the steering wheel.

'You did,' Carla replies, matter of fact.

Jake looks up. 'I need to tell her I'm sorry. Make it better.'

Carla says nothing. Taps the pocket of her jeans and lifts her hips from the seat to squeeze out a squashed packet of cigarettes.

'I...' Jake starts.

'You were mad. I should have told you about me and Sandy. It was just hard... I knew you wouldn't like it.' She offers a cigarette from her packet to Jake.

He shakes his head.

Carla winds down the window and lights the cigarette. She blows a gust of smoke out the window and rubs her other hand on her thigh. The denim makes a scratchy sound under her nails.

'I hate it when you're like this,' she says.

'Like what?' Jake says without tone.

'Like...' She looks around her, searching for the word, holds her palms to the sky. 'So... so... defeated.'

'What the fuck does that mean?' he huffs.

She shrugs. 'It wasn't really about Sandy. Why I left.'

He doesn't answer. He winds down his window, the cigarette smell sickening him.

'It was lots of things,' she continues. 'I changed. You

changed. Your mum hated me. I hated Stinky Gully. I felt like I was in a box. I needed to get out. Be myself again.'

Jake fiddles with the keys. Takes them out of the ignition. Puts them back in.

'Remember...' he says.

Carla taps ash out of the window.

'Remember...' he says, and groans.

'Remember what?' She looks at him, her eyes in shadow.

'Remember when we first met?' he says.

She smiles slightly and touches his hand. 'They were good times. Good memories.'

He pulls his hand away. Tucks it under his thigh.

'Remember the baby? The other baby.'

'It wasn't a baby.' She won't look at him now. She stares out the window at the black river. 'It was as tiny as a pin head. A group of cells. You can't make me... that was years ago.'

'Don't you ever wonder...'

'I couldn't have had a baby then!' She spins around, her voice high. 'It wasn't the right time. You weren't ready. You said so.'

'I never said that.'

'You didn't *have* to say it!'

He breathes deeply and expels the air over the dash. 'I should have said... I should have said I wanted it. I did want it.'

She looks away again, taking a deep drag of her cigarette.

'Fuck it.' He slaps the steering wheel. 'Don't you think about it? How old he would be? What he would be doing now?'

'He?' she says out the window.

'I always thought it was a he,' Jake says.

She pushes fingers into her temples.

'Maybe if you told me,' he continues, 'talked to me. Instead of just going off and doing what you wanted and not telling me till it was done.'

'It! It's called a termination.'

'Abortion,' he spits back.

She flicks her cigarette out the window. It glows briefly on the footpath. 'Sorry,' she says, barely audible. 'I didn't know you still thought about it.'

'Whatever.' He shuffles in his seat, taps the outside of the car with his nails. 'I was wondering. Can I take La-Li to Mum's tomorrow?'

'I was thinking about that girl that went missing in Stinky Gully,' she says in reply.

The sinking lost feeling from the city footpath descends on Jake.

Carla continues. 'I think I remember her—from day care when we lived out there. Her mum did house cleaning. We talked about her doing our place but… I don't know, she was bit skanky. I wasn't sure I wanted her in my house.'

Jake's teeth grind together.

'I can't imagine how she feels now. How it is to not know where your little girl is,' Carla says.

Jake heaves.

'Jake?'

Jake's breath shudders. 'I saw her. The girl.'

'What?'

'On Sunday, when I stopped for petrol. She was getting into a car.'

Carla leans toward him. 'You told the police?'

'I told the police.'

'And?'

'I don't know… I didn't know they were looking for her. I just came from there… The cop station. What if she's dead because I didn't…' His words fall into a bundle of sobs.

Carla lifts herself in her seat and twists over him. She

reaches her arms around him and hugs his shoulders. 'It's not your fault,' she whispers.

The warmth of her, the familiarity, like a feather-filled doona on a winter's night.

She pulls back a little and he sees her face shining with tears. He leans in, the desire for her mouth, his and her mouth together. So close, her breathing the same breath as him. She springs away.

He sinks into his seat, his heart, his chest concave to his spine. A wind slaps the trees and their leaves crunch fists against each other.

'We should go back,' Carla says.

They drive back in silence.

Jake stops at front of her house. Turns off the ignition.

He stares straight ahead. 'Can I come get La-Li tomorrow? In the afternoon? Take her to Mum's place?'

Carla opens the car door. 'I'll talk to her. See if that is what she wants. I'll call.' She swings her feet out of the car.

'My phone is flat,' Jake says.

'Charge it then.' She shakes her head.

Sandy appears like an apparition at the gate. Carla holds up her hand. Sandy stops like an obedient dog.

'Jake,' she says.

'What?' His hand is on the ignition.

'What do you really want?'

His hand drops. He looks at the warm glow of the house. Sandy at the gate like a yapping bull dog on a lead.

'I want La-Li. I want you... you... how it was. Before.'

Carla scrapes her feet on the bitumen; it crunches like bones. 'That's not going to happen, Jake,' she says. 'You need to think about what you want for *you*.'

A night time and almost a whole day happens. He comes and goes, pokes and prods her. One time he says it takes three days to die of thirst, he reckons—what does she think? Another time he says: Eloise didn't hear a thing, deaf bitch.

The puppy comes and goes and rests against her face, snuggles into her neck and yawns, silent mouth wide and gummy. Baby doesn't speak. Baby never talked at all. The Magic was pretend. She is alone. Only a puppy that is a ghost and not real. Just a thing her mind made up.

She wishes he was real. But if he was real, he would be dead by now. One kick from *him* would kill a little puppy. Mr Randall. Not a stick monster. A real man. A real man a bit dumb in the head. Declan is probably smarter than he is. Declan can read better. Because, she thinks, when he says he lost his glasses he is pretending because he doesn't want to say he can't read. All grown-ups should be able to read. They have been to school for years and years, not just one year like her. She can read better than him and she has only done Prep. Even though she is not very good at Prep and Rachel is lots smarter.

Who will Rachel be best friends with now? Will Rachel miss her? On the first day of grade one will she go to school and wonder where Bree-Anna is and sit by herself and eat lunch? She has been best friends with Rachel since the first day. Bree-Anna saw, when they unpacked their books and crayons into their desks, that they had the same pencil case. The same pink pencil case. And then she saw they both had the same lunch box! Pink! She was scared of school. The noise and the boys and the teachers. She could barely remember how to talk, her mouth stuck together with fear. She remembered what Grandma said. She remembers remembering it. She had that feeling, in her tummy, all churny and gluggy, but a tickle like excitement too and she thought, it is just like the big pool. Being scared makes you braver. So she went, on purpose, to

Rachel. Maybe she won't like me, she had thought, but she found a brave and said, 'Look, we've got the same lunch box and the same pencil case.' And that was it. They were best friends. Forever. Until now, when she will be dead soon.

At least she doesn't have to worry about Baby anymore. But she does miss her.

She will miss Mummy and Grandma too. And Declan. Declan might miss her. Declan says she is a pest and dumb, but sometimes, like one time when some big boys were teasing and throwing sand at her, he said leave her alone. And he gave her those books. The ones he didn't want anymore. Anyway, she was dumb and a pest. Dumber than Declan, who got best marks for maths.

Her brain is thinking. She can't do sleep anymore, she wants to think. Think about all the things she doesn't want to forget like her favourite shows and her favourite movies. Thinking of these things makes her forget how the tape itches and hurts and how her fingers and hands throb and tingle. She can't think so it comes like a dream. A floaty dream and she is not really here. He could make her be tied up and die but he couldn't make her think what he wanted. She could think whatever she wanted.

Where is *he?*

The TV got dragged out of the bedroom. She kind of remembers that. And she heard it sometimes, in her dreaming, in the other room. It is quiet now. He might have gone to the shops. Tomorrow is Christmas Day. Today is Christmas Eve. Maybe. If she counted right. Santa will have already got stuff ready for her. But she won't need it. If she could wish to Santa, she would say to give her presents to Rachel instead. Prickles come up her body like she is going to cry, but there is no water left in her.

She was brave when she talked to Rachel the first time.

If Declan was here, he would have escaped. He would have figured out how to open the window and he would have jumped and run all the way to the shops. But then, Declan wouldn't have been stupid enough to think Mr Randall was friends with Rachel and would be going to her party.

If there was one thing she could change in her life, it would be believing Mr Randall when he said that.

She would have kept on walking. That might have taken some brave. Or she would have turned around and gone the other way. Or not left home at all. Been braver about the dreadlock man she used to think was a troll, but was just a man who was not very nice. She didn't know if he was smart or stupid like Mr Randall but he was definitely not nice.

They drove past a graveyard sometimes. Just on the outside of town near all the new houses. Is that where they would put her? After they found her in the bush where he said he would leave her. Being in the bush scared her. It would be dark and there would be wild animals and they might eat her. But she would be dead so she wouldn't feel it. Her ghost might watch. If she comes back as a ghost she is going to come back and haunt Mr Randall. Make him go crazy with sorry. She would find a way to leave clues so the policemans come and arrest him and he goes to jail. She would really like the policemans to find out what he did to her. He could go to jail. He said that. He knows that. That is why he is letting her die of thirst. What he did to her, taking her away without asking Mummy, was wrong enough for him to go to jail.

She is thirsty.

A glass of water.

A bottle of water.

A whole tank of water.

And a pair of scissors to cut the tape off her aching hands.

She would be a brave ghost. It would be like how she felt

after she kicked him where it hurt. It was brave, she didn't really think of it at the time, to kick him. And she was scared after. But it felt good too because she hurt him and she saved herself from him seeing under her nightie. And maybe saved herself from him touching her like the dreadlock troll did before Declan came and scared him. Declan was brave that morning, she realises. He could have just gone away, but he said something and scared the dreadlock troll man.

She was braver when she first got here. Asking where the toilet was and asking for him to take her home. That was before he lied to her about Mummy coming and before she knew that he liked to kick and hurt. She got more scared instead of more brave.

She remembers.

He didn't use scissors.

He used his teeth.

He ripped the tape with his teeth. It went snap!

She twists her hands up to her face. Her shoulders groan with pain and she thinks she will have one hell of a bruise. Lots of them.

She grips the edge of the tape with her sharp teeth. Not her front teeth for biting, not her back teeth for chewing, the ones in between she used when Grandma showed her how to sew and she cut the cotton with her teeth and Grandma said, *Don't use your teeth.*

She saws with her teeth back and forth across the tape like she is a mouse chewing slowly to make a hole in a packet of sugar. A bit comes off! She spits it out.

Her heart beats fast. She grinds her teeth against the edge of the tape again and *chomp*! Another rip in the tape.

The door bangs on the wall when he flings it open. She jumps, pulls her hands from her mouth. So he can't see what she is doing.

He walks to her feet. Nudges her soles. She keeps still. Still as a statue. Frozen.

He walks around the front of her. Pokes her belly with his foot. She breathes a big grumbly breath. Makes it so he can see she is still breathing. She doesn't want him to take her to the bush. To think she is dead. She wants him to think she is sleeping. Almost dead but not quite. Then he will leave her alone. Let her die of thirst some more. And she can chew chew chew on the tape.

She is smarter than him.

She hears him sit on the end of the bed. He is watching her. She can feel his eyes on her, though her eyes are closed. She can hear mice in the walls. She can hear the fridge popping into life. She can hear the rumble of his hungry belly. She can hear the whizz of cars on the road outside. She can hear the squawk of crows and far away thunder. She can hear grasshoppers eating grass.

She can hear her heart going *bang bang* alive in her chest.

He will get bored watching her. She knows him.

He will get up and watch TV. That is what he does. She must be boring. Too boring for him to stay and watch.

She makes it so her breathing is little, like a dying person. But not dead yet.

Lightning lights the room, bright like the middle of the day. The thunder is closer, shaking the house with its big hands. It doesn't scare her.

Before he leaves the room, he kicks her three times, between her shoulders. Kick, kick, kick. Bree-Anna grits her teeth, shuts her eyes, and holds her breath so as not to make a noise. A noise would make him think she is too alive and needs more kicking for her to die. She could cut off his legs. Cut off his feet. He is so mean when he kicks.

The door stays open. The TV snaps awake like she knew it would.

Slow and sneaky she lifts her hands to her mouth. She finds the edge of the tape and scrapes her teeth back and forth. Her teeth slip and slip across the skin on her hands. She searches for the tape again; her teeth grab and pull at the tiny hairs on her wrists until she finds the edge of the tape. Her heavy breath grunts gusts in short bursts across her hands. Is she too loud? She stops. Freezes and listens. The television laughs and she hears him laugh back and move on the couch but not get up.

It takes forever, and her jaw aches and clicks. Rain smashes the roof and the wind howls and she is glad of its noise. She runs out of breath, runs out of saliva to swallow, runs out of saliva to spit the crumbs of red tape. What would she do when she finished? What if he finds her, hands free? She doesn't know. She just keeps on chewing. Chews faster, her heart beating faster. Racing his curiosity, his boredom. Whatever it is that gave him the idea to come and look at her, kick her.

The rain gets quieter and then stops. The TV flickers from the next room.

The tape becomes loose enough for her to pull her hands apart and *snap*! The rest of the tape bursts apart.

She lies still on the floral carpet, smells its dust tickle her nose. Listens. The television drones and shifts loud to quiet and music to voices.

'Fuck you, bitch!' he shouts, and she feels a trickle of pee between her legs. But it is the TV he shouts at and the channel changes—*click, click, click*—until it settles in one place again.

She sits slowly, a gasp of pain escapes, but she clamps her hand over her mouth and tells herself to shut up. Just shut up and be quiet. Her hands slip around the tape around her ankles. Feeling for an end, the line in the smoothness that shows this is where the tape ends. She can't find it! *Mummy*, she whimpers, and tears burn her eyes. Mummy always finds the end of the tape when she can't. But Mummy is not here. Mummy is frantic with worry. If she doesn't get home, she will think she is dead. Like everyone else thinks.

She will be. She will be. She will be dead. Dead is the end. She stops her searching and closes her eyes. Haste makes waste, Grandma says. She touches the tape slowly, slow as a caterpillar eating a leaf. She will only find the end if she touches all the tape. Feels every part of it. There it is, the rough, crinkled end. She picks at it with her nail. Loses it. Wails silent tears and starts again. Finds it, picks at it, lifts it away, winds the tape around and around, freeing her feet.

Now she can stand. She rushes to her feet. The window. But dizziness overwhelms her and she falls against the bed and squeals. No, no, *NO*. She stops, still leaning on the bed. Her head aches. It feels like someone is smashing her head with a brick.

The TV plays on. The wind rustles the trees.

She feels her way along the bed; the room grows bigger and smaller with each throb of her head. Can she remember how to open the window?

At the top of the bed, she feels for the wall, finds only air and then almost falls into the wall when she finds it. She runs her hands over the wall, into the dips and grooves until the bump of the windowsill forms beneath them.

She can't reach high enough to push the top part where she needs to push. The chair against the wall seems so far away. She wobbles toward it, leaving the support of the wall and tumbles against it so it holds her up. She drags it across the carpet, no longer caring about being quiet. She just wants out. Out.

The chair in front of the window, she climbs on top of it. Shoves her hands at the top of the window. Every muscle in her body, the weight of her body pushes on the window and *chink*! It lifts. She grunts and heaves it higher. She lifts herself to sit on the windowsill and feels blindly for the metal lever to hold the window open. She can't find it! Haste makes waste, she tells herself again. The window heavy in her hand, she rests it on her shoulder and it digs heavy into her.

'Hey!'

He fills the doorway. His steps the size of giants, he comes toward her. She turns her legs, through the window, and jumps.

Her feet hit the ground with a jolt that goes all the way up her before she falls and her elbows slam onto the wet dirt.

She doesn't look up. Doesn't wait to see if he is at the window. She claws along the ground until she is on her feet. All her pain gone, she flies across the ground, through bushes and leaves that flick water on her and—*smack*—into a wooden fence.

She grabs the splintered fence palings between her hands and rattles them. Her skin bursts with electricity. The fence trembles and sways.

'You cunt. You little cunt, get back here.'

She stumbles along the fence, deeper to the back of the yard, where it's darker and more tangled. Her hand *bump bump bumps* over each paling until it plunges through a gap, a broken fallen part of the fence.

She glances behind her, then puts first a leg and an arm through the gap. She squeezes her stomach tight, pulls it in, her chest expanding. She's too fat. She's stuck. One arm, one leg in his garden, one arm, one leg in the long grass. She sobs and struggles but can't move.

'Where are you?' The garden swishes with his movements —or is it the wind?

She sniffs in a breath and heaves; her skin rips through the gap and she collapses into the long, wet grass.

She shuffles through the grass on her hands and knees until her legs dig deep into the mud and her body lifts and she runs, the grass whipping at her face, slicing her arms, the air behind her pushing her faster, faster toward the light of the car park and—*smack*—into another fence.

But she knows where this fence ends. Panting, she runs toward the road, car headlights bright across its surface. The fence ends, and she spins around it into the garden that fronts the car park. She stops, all the breath squeezed out of her; the pain of her bruises, the throbbing of her head returns. She looks back at his house. The lights of his froggy car bump down his driveway and she must keep running.

She sprints across the car park. A lady pushes a trolley. A man huddles, packing groceries into the boot. She calls out, 'Help me,' but it is like she has no voice and she is not there at all. They don't see her, and for an instant she wonders if she is a ghost already. She ducks between cars and out again, weaves her way up onto the concrete at the front of Woolworth's.

People inside the supermarket move around, silent behind the glass. A baby in a shopping trolley waves a biscuit at her. She doesn't recognise anyone. What should she do? Ask someone for help? What if they don't believe her? She realises she hoped, expected, to get here and Mummy would be waiting.

She twists around. The froggy car is parked in the first row. She turns in a panicked circle. Where is he? She heaves deep breaths and tears well up like an ocean. She can't see him anywhere. She scrambles down on her hands and knees and crawls under the seat outside the newsagent. She locks herself into a tight ball as invisible as she can be.

When he finds her, what will he do? Pick her up and carry

her back to his froggy car and back to his mother's bedroom with the giant bed and tape her up with better tape and kick her and...

His feet, she knows his ugly yellow toenails.

His feet stop by the seat. Right by her. She closes her eyes. She buries her head in her knees. Goodbye Mummy. Goodbye Grandma. Goodbye Declan.

A big hand lands on her shoulder and she screams.

But it isn't his face.

'Are you Bree-Anna?'

It is the newsagent man. The one Mummy cleans for.

CHRISTMAS DAY

Jake's brother lends him a phone charger that fits his phone. He has a stash of chargers and computer leads that outweighs his actual phone and computer ownership.

La-Li's voice scratches on the other end of the phone. He apologises. He says he would never hurt her. He says it was wrong of him to lose his temper.

She says, 'That's what Mummy said.' She says, 'Mummy got angry when I threw my dinner once. I've tried real hard since then, even when I don't like what Sandy cooks me.'

'Will you forgive me?' he asks.

'If you try harder, Daddy,' she says. 'Count to ten. That's what I do.'

Christmas Day beats heat into his mother's house. The cream on the trifle glistens with a sheen of milky sweat. His mother bought a gift for La-Li and the gift tag, a kangaroo in the desert with a Santa hat, says *To La-Li, Love from Daddy.*

La-Li picks at each piece of sticky tape and reveals the gift slowly, like sucking on a lollipop all day. Jake thinks about the missing girl. Wonders what her family is doing today. If they have unwrapped gifts under a tree. If the girl was—is—a ripper of paper or a takes-her-time like La-Li.

The gift is a doll's house. Jake has to build it. They do it together and he asks La-Li if she wants to build a real house with him one day.

'Yes,' she says. 'One in the bush, with a creek you can swim in. Like you said once.'

He forgot he told her about that. The house, it didn't have to be flash land, scrubby and rugged, he didn't want to grow anything other than a home. And a shed. With classic cars he would fix for other people and maybe collect himself.

Later in the twilight, La-Li makes up stories in the kitchen of her new doll's house, the little dolls bobbing and talking to each other. The neighbours have been and gone and demolished the Camembert. His mother sleeps off the Riesling and his brother retires to his room to kill zombies or enemy soldiers. Jake uses his phone to search the job sites. There's some jobs in the meat works close to Carla's house that raises his hopes. He's done that sort of work before.

Then he turns to the real estate sites. It doesn't have to be good land—sandy, rocky, scrubby, it doesn't matter—just so long as it has a nice flat space for a house and a shed.

The newsagent man took her to the back of his shop and got the shop girl to get her a green slushie. For free. She couldn't drink it though. It made her sick. The policemans came and then an ambulance and they took her in the ambulance and she wanted Mummy and what she didn't know was Mummy was following in the car.

At the hospital, Mummy got her hand and squeezed it and never let go so her hand got sweaty and squashed. They gave her a drip, which didn't drip at all but was a needle in her arm. They tested her bones and x-rayed her and used machines and said severe bruising and a miracle nothing was broken or damaged. The policemans came, and she told them about Mr Randall taking her to his house. About how she rang up and left a message and Mummy said, I didn't know, I didn't hear it, and squeezed her hand more and cried. They wanted to look at her more and Mummy kept shaking her head and crying and saying I can't stand it, not that, and they called it a rape kit and then they gave her a needle and she went to sleep.

She woke in the morning and Mummy still held her hand like she would never let it go, but Bree-Anna knew she would have to one day. They wanted to keep her for observing. Mummy said enough is enough and it's Christmas Day, and they let her go home. They didn't want her to go home. But Mummy made them. In the car, it smelled like it always used to, before she was at Mr Randall's. She curled in a ball on the back seat, her seatbelt on, and fell asleep.

When she wakes, it takes a minute to work out where she is. The cool room hums with air-conditioning and she remembers. Mummy isn't there, but the smell of her and the shape where her head rested in the pillow are still there. She can't remember getting home. Mummy must have carried her to the bed.

It is still Christmas, but she doesn't get up. She hugs Mummy's pillow close and drifts back into sleep.

Next time she wakes, Mummy is there. Mummy wraps her arms around her and says she is the best Christmas present ever. She lets her go and wipes Bree-Anna's fringe from her forehead.

'You need a bath.' She laughs.

Bree-Anna smiles and nods and the muscles on the back of her neck stretch and ache and tears start to come.

Mummy wipes them away. 'Are you hungry?'

'Starving,' Bree-Anna whispers, because talking louder is too much energy.

'Do you want to eat here or come out to the loungeroom?'

'Come out,' Bree-Anna says.

But Mummy doesn't get off the bed. Instead, she stares at the curtains and taps her fingers against her thigh and then she says, 'I don't want you to worry about Colin Randall. The police put him in jail. He can't hurt you anymore. He can't get you or any other little girls.'

But she isn't worried about Mr Randall. She is never going to get in a car with him again. But she figures, it is a good thing no other little girl would be tricked into his froggy car either.

She sits up and Mummy puts a pillow behind her back.

'How's that?'

She nods, though really her shoulders hurt when she moves and her head aches.

If he is not there, then the house is empty. 'Can we go and get Baby?'

'Baby? Your doll?'

Bree-Anna nods and fights the urge to put her thumb in her mouth. 'She's still at Mr Randall's house.'

Mummy leans over and plumps the pillow with her fists. 'The police won't let us get Baby right now.'

'The policemans have Baby?'

'Yes, she is with the policemans,' Mummy says.

Tears burst from her eyes and Mummy says again don't worry he can't hurt you. But she's crying because it's not fair, Baby shouldn't be in jail, but she doesn't know how to say so.

'I want Baby,' Bree-Anna says.

'We'll get you another doll,' she says and Bree-Anna shakes her head and puts her thumb in her mouth. Tears wet her face.

Mummy grabs her and squeezes hard, hurting all her

bruises. 'Okay, the police will bring her home. I will tell them. She is just on an adventure first.' She pulls away and looks at Bree-Anna. 'Okay?'

Bree-Anna thinks Baby has had enough adventures, but she doesn't say so. And how did the police know that she was in the suitcase, anyway? She doesn't think the police have her at all and it is one of those lies that grown-ups tell so you will stop asking.

Then she remembers Baby is only a doll and feels even sadder.

Mummy runs her a bath and cries and touches the blue bruises on her body. She washes her all over, trying her best not to hurt her. It still hurts, but Bree-Anna tries hard not to cry.

It is a long time past waking up early to open presents and Declan has had to wait. He doesn't complain. She sits on the couch and he brings all her presents to her. Mummy keeps bringing her more food. Healthy things, she says, like the hospital said. They are food in little plastic boxes that are called frozen dinners. Bree-Anna has never seen food like them before. And she should keep her liquids up, so there is water and then some Fanta.

Clean and not hungry anymore, Bree-Anna lies on the couch, her new iPad beside her. She can't find the energy to play it.

The phone rings and she overhears Mummy talking to Grandma about coming for a late Christmas dinner.

'Grandma has a special surprise for you,' Mummy says, but it is not really a surprise because she heard her Mummy say a kitten was all right but she wasn't going to deal with walking a dog every day.

Somehow, she knows the attention she is getting won't last forever.

Someone knocks on the door and Bree-Anna sits up excited. Grandma!

But the face at the door is not Grandma, it is the ugly dreadlock man that she used to think was a troll. Bree-Anna's stomach sinks—everything is spoiled already. He ruffles her hair and says it's good to see her safe and sound, and Mummy hugs him and says he is to stay for late Christmas dinner, it's not much, just what she could find in the house and a chicken a nice neighbour gave her to roast. It is just about finished and ready to serve, if her mother ever gets here. She means Grandma.

Bree-Anna slinks into the kitchen and stands at the door, watching them. Mummy stands at the stove stirring gravy and he goes behind her and rubs himself on her and makes Mummy giggle and turn and slap him, but not to hurt him. He leaves Mummy alone and sits at the table. He opens a packet of cigarettes and takes one out. He taps it on the table and notices her at the door. He winks at her. Bree-Anna puts her thumb in her mouth and leans on the door frame. He searches his pockets and pulls out a lighter and lights the cigarette, sucking hard on the end and blowing rings of smoke at the ceiling.

'I think there's a beer in the fridge,' Mummy calls over her shoulder and takes the saucepan off the stove.

'Right on,' he says and twists in his chair to reach the fridge. He gets the beer and turns back to the table, puts the cigarette in his mouth, and holds it there while he turns the beer cap. He throws the lid on the table, sucks smoke out of the cigarette and blows into the air, then drinks a huge drink of beer.

Mummy turns and smiles at him and sees that she is at the door.

'What's wrong, honey?' she asks.

Bree-Anna shakes her head.

'You're tired, honey. Don't stand there, go and lie down. Food will be ready soon. Roast chicken, veggies, gravy.'

Bree-Anna turns and heads back to the loungeroom. On the couch she rests a pillow on her lap, places the iPad on it, stares at it and waits.

He comes in. She knew he would. He puts his beer on the coffee table and grins at her. His teeth are yellow on the edges, near his gums, and she can't imagine how Mummy wants to kiss him.

'It's good you're back,' he says. 'Your mum was worried about you.'

She doesn't look at him. Stares at her iPad.

'You got an iPad? Is that your Christmas present? What games do you have?' He reaches over and takes it from her and turns it on.

'There's nothing on it,' he says. 'You haven't downloaded any games?'

She doesn't answer. Looks at the Christmas tree lights winking and blinking red, blue, green. Her thumb goes in her mouth.

He rests his hand on her leg, under the pillow on her lap. Her insides cringe and crinkle.

'You got games?'

He runs his hand up and down her leg, like he's patting a dog or a kitten.

Sickness flows through her; she remembers Mr Randall, but she remembers him too. Like a troll in her bedroom.

'Where are the games?' he says, leaning in closer to her ear. His breath on her. In her.

She turns and looks at him fierce and says, her teeth gritted, 'Don't touch me,' and she didn't know her voice could sound so deep and grumbly.

He takes his hand away.

Mummy comes out and says food is ready and they just have to wait for her mum, but he says I'm going, and she says but dinner, and she grabs his elbow and says stay Glen, please, and pulls him toward the kitchen, but he just kisses her on the cheek and she follows him to the door.

He goes out the door and Mummy closes it. Real quiet and soft. Sad, not angry, but Bree-Anna knows Mummy is better off without him. He is not a nice man.

The traditional Christmas photo in Eloise's house has changed over time. From the early photos of just Anthony as a baby, then both of them, growing from toddlers to teenagers, always on the floor in front of the tree surrounded by the trappings and wrappings of the commercialisation of Christmas. Boxes and presents cocooning them, anticipation on their faces as children, despair and embarrassment as hormones and acne rained down on them. Their mother keeps them all in one album together. Like a timeline of family togetherness turning slowly to ruin. It's been a few years since one was taken and Eloise's mother seems surprised when she suggests they all pose for a photo.

'Yes, let's bring that tradition back,' her mother says. Eloise realises she had a thought of the photo as full stop, the last page in the album.

'Nice camera,' her brother says when she brings it out of her room. 'Give us a look.'

'Get your beady little eyes off it,' her father says. It's one of his lucid days.

'I just want to look,' Anthony says. All morning they've alternated between bickering and doting. Eloise feels like she is balancing on a barbed-wire fence, her feet bleeding from the barbs, but not sure which way to jump.

'Sit in front of the tree,' she says. They drag over dining room chairs and she sets up the tripod and watches them through the lens. 'Mum, we're ready,' she calls. The phone rings.

'Just leave it,' her father says. Eloise focuses in closer and snaps his grumpy face. 'It's probably someone selling something.'

'Not on Christmas Day, that's stupid,' Anthony says.

Eloise snaps the shutter, the digital camera taking lightning fast photos of her father's change from grumpy, burning embarrassment to glaring anger. She stops and looks up at the two of them.

'Are you taking photos already?' Anthony asks.

'No,' Eloise says.

'Is this for your portfolio?' Anthony asks, baiting her.

'What portfolio?' their father says.

'Sit still,' Eloise says and returns to seeing him through the lens.

'They found Bree-Anna!'

Eloise's stomach lurches.

'Where was she?' Eloise asks. 'Who said?'

'Amber's mother. She rang to say she turned up last night, at the shops.'

'In Stinky Gully?' her father says. 'How could she be lost at those shops? That's ridiculous, woman. You've got your wires crossed.'

'No—she escaped. She was at that Randall boy's house. He snatched her and he's been keeping her there.'

Eloise's stomach tightens. 'Is she all right? Did he hurt her?'

Her mother comes and puts her arm around her shoulder. 'She's going to be fine.'

'Don't you clean for that Randall kid?' her father chips in. 'Weren't you just there Tuesday?'

How come his memory doesn't fail him now?

'Eloise?' her brother says.

'I rang the police last night,' she says. 'I told them about Colin.'

'You knew she was there?' Her mother's arms drop from her shoulder. 'You didn't say anything?'

'No,' Eloise says, 'I just had a funny feeling something wasn't right. It took me a while to put it together.' Tears start to build in her eyes. 'I should have figured it out on Tuesday. They could have got there sooner. She escaped?'

'Jumped out a window and ran apparently,' her mother says.

Eloise covers her mouth with her hand, her tears no longer able to hide.

'Oh, come on,' her mother says, pulling a tissue from her pocket and giving it to Eloise. 'Don't blame yourself. You weren't to know.'

'What's this about a bloody portfolio?' her father says again.

'Yeah,' Anthony chimes in. 'You putting a portfolio together or something? Are you keeping secrets from your father, Eloise?'

Eloise wants to punch and hug him.

She wipes the tears from her face, the snot from the end of her nose. 'I'll go and get it,' she says and leaves the camera waiting.

ACKNOWLEDGMENTS

I respectfully acknowledge the Traditional Owners of the land on which this book was imagined, the Yuggera and Ugarapul people. I pay my respects to Elders past, present, and future. I recognise the Aboriginal and Torres Strait Islander peoples as the first storytellers of this nation and the significance of storytelling in Aboriginal and Torres Strait Islander peoples' unique relationship to land, water, and seas.

Stinky Gully is named for the real place of Stinking Gully, a town now known as Fernvale. Land that was never ceded. In the early 1800s, so-called explorers 'discovered' the Brisbane Valley. Wealthy pastoralists followed in the 1840s and selectors in the 1860s. The hunger for cotton led to the establishment of large cotton gin in Stinking Gully. My German ancestors settled in Queensland too, somewhat west of Fernvale where I now live. As a child, I was never taught or told stories of the frontier wars that occurred when Aboriginal peoples fought against our invasion. We believed the myth of a peaceful settlement.

The white settlements at Stinking Gully and Fernvale were founded as a result of the violent dispossession of Aboriginal people. By acknowledging our history of atrocities, my heartfelt hope is that we create a space for healing and the power to change the colonial structures that continue to disadvantage and cause violence to Aboriginal and Torres Strait Islander peoples.

If you know Fernvale, you will recognise some of the places in my book, but I promise you won't recognise anyone. You are not in my book. Your local supermarket is in the book. Thank you to the place I live for inspiring me to imagine Bree-Anna, Jake, Eloise, and Colin Randall.

Thank you to my early readers, the members of the Writers and Critters group, and my daughter Miriama. Thank you to my family for allowing me to disappear into a room and head-space for writing. Thank you to my publisher Michelle Lovi and Odyssey Books for continuing to create an opportunity to send my work into the world. All my books are my babies, and this third baby is known to me as *Baby*. Thank you for reading.

ABOUT THE AUTHOR

When Kathryn Gossow started writing, she was told to choose a genre and stick to it. In the same way that she ignored her grade 9 science teacher, she ignored this advice. Her first novel, Aurelias short-listed *Cassandra,* is mythic fiction retelling; her second book, *The Dark Poet,* is a collection of gritty short stories about the dangers of charismatic men. In real life, Kathryn loves many things: jonquils, decaying buildings, sarsaparilla, lemon curd, cold winds, warm spring days, music festivals. True Crime. The ordinariness of life meeting the extraordinary of crime. From this obsession springs her third book, a small-town thriller, *Taking Baby for a Walk.* Kathryn is a co-editor of *South of the Sun: Australian Fairy Tales for the 21st Century* anthology and a keen explorer of fairy tales. She adores flash fiction and has a number of short stories out in the world.

www.kathryngossow.net.au

ALSO BY KATHRYN GOSSOW

Cassandra

The Dark Poet